NO. AR.

MVFOL

Cilla Lee-Jenkins

THE EPIC STORY

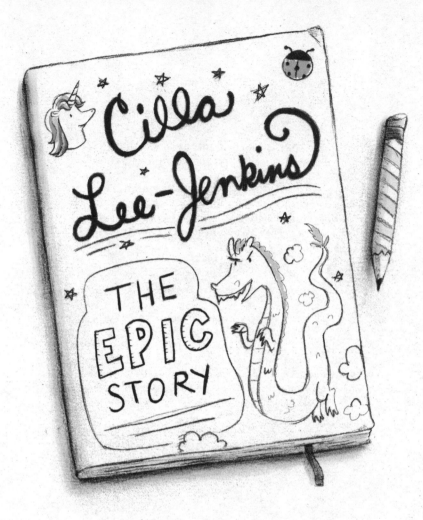

BY SUSAN TAN

ILLUSTRATED BY DANA WULFEKOTTE

Roaring Brook Press
New York

Text copyright © 2019 by Susan Tan
Illustrations copyright © 2019 by Dana Wulfekotte

Published by Roaring Brook Press
Roaring Brook Press is a division of
Holtzbrinck Publishing Holdings Limited Partnership
175 Fifth Avenue, New York, NY 10010

mackids.com

Library of Congress Control Number: 2018944828
ISBN: 978-1-250-18363-7

Our books may be purchased in bulk for promotional, educational,
or business use. Please contact your local bookseller or the Macmillan
Corporate and Premium Sales Department at (800) 221-7945 ext. 5442 or
by email at MacmillanSpecialMarkets@macmillan.com.

First edition, 2019
Book design by Aimee Fleck
Printed in the United States of America by
LSC Communications, Harrisonburg, Virginia

1   3   5   7   9   10   8   6   4   2

To Dad,
Bobby,
Ye Ye,
and Uncle Paul.
You speak my language.

AN (EPIC) START

Let me tell you, oh reader, of Cilla Lee-Jenkins.
Future author, destiny great.
Her fate in middle school will hopefully be an
  excellent one,
And everyone will like her, and will be impressed
  by how grown-up she is.
The end.

Hi. **That kind of beginning—with fancy** language, and almost poetry, and saying "oh" when you talk to someone—is how you start an Epic.

Which is what this book is.

An Epic, as you can maybe tell from the word, is a REALLY exciting kind of story, all about Adventure and Fate. Epics have lots of Drama (which I love). They involve some sort of Quest, and usually there are Struggles to overcome, or an enemy to vanquish. Epic heroes perform Feats, like defeating (or making friends with) dragons, or saving the world.

The best part about deciding to write an Epic is that there are so many different kinds. Some Epics are about ancient times and involve traveling on stormy seas, and fighting with swords, and wrestling bears, and whatever else people used to do back then. Other Epics, though, are set in space and involve giant laser beam battles and evil alien slugs. Even lots of superhero books are Epics (especially when a hero has to save the world from being blown up, or turned to molten lava, which happens a lot in superhero stories).

My Epic probably won't have bears or dragons, which is too bad. But it will be about something just as scary. Because this is the Epic story of my last year in elementary school.

It all began on the first day of fifth grade, when Ms. Paradise gave us each a packet of forms to take home to our parents. Right on top was a Very

Official-Looking, Serious letter. It wasn't the exciting kind, with a message telling me I'm about to inherit magical powers and need to go fulfill my destiny, like in the books.

But a letter about middle school.

And how I need to start getting ready for it.

I'm a little (or a lot) nervous about middle school. It's much bigger than my school now, and there are older kids there. Instead of having one classroom I'll have a different one for every subject, with a different teacher, too (which seems excessive). And apparently there will be a lot of Expectations. Expectations about knowing all the times tables, and having total Focus in class, and, worst of all, being Serious and grown-up ALL THE TIME.

Everyone seems to be excited about middle school, not nervous like me. Even Colleen (my best friend!) is happy to go and says things like "I can't wait!" or "One more year!" So I don't know how to tell her that I CAN wait. In fact, I'm happy to wait a long time.

All this could make for a very hard year. But don't worry. Luckily, I'm not just any fifth grader.

I'm destined for greatness as a future author extraordinaire.

And I know how to take destiny into my own hands.

Because the most important thing about an Epic is that there is *always* a happy ending. No matter how much you Struggle, if you're in one, you know you'll emerge victorious. By the end you'll have won the treasure, or become queen of a kingdom, or made a new dragon friend. And afterward, everyone will know about your victories and say, "Wow, she's so amazing and mature!" when you pass by.

Which would be wonderful.

Even though my Epic will be a little different because I get seasick on boat rides, am scared of slugs, and don't have superpowers (unfortunately), I know it will still end in the same way.

And when my Epic is done, I should be ready to be a middle schooler.

This book won't just be about overcoming Epic Struggles, though. There will be Adventures, too, and I have TONS to tell you because last year, I didn't write a book at all. So you have lots to look forward to, and I'll introduce you to my friends, and family, and favorite new stories. And, of course, you'll also meet the Foes in my life (they're very important for an Epic, especially when it comes to defeating them).

Imagine me soaring off to save the world, my cape flapping out behind me. Or at the front of a ship, heading off into stormy seas and unknown dangers (probably involving at least one dragon, hopefully two).

I hope you enjoy our Adventure.

Sincerely,
Your friend
and hopefully soon-to-be Epic hero,

CILLA LEE-JENKINS
Future Author Extraordinaire

1

OVERHEARD IN FIFTH GRADE

My Epic Quest begins in fifth grade, right around the time I realized that despite its name, Ms. Paradise's class is no paradise.

I used to be something called Literal, which means I thought words meant exactly what they sounded like. For example, I'd get upset when my mom said things like "I'm so hungry, I could eat a horse" because no, Mom, horses are our friends, and there's plenty of food in the refrigerator, and WHY WOULD YOU DO SUCH A THING?!

But now I know this is just an expression. So when my mom says this, she just means she's really hungry. Understanding expressions has made life a lot easier (though I still don't quite understand why adults can't just say what they mean, but that's a separate issue).

So I wasn't expecting Ms. Paradise's class to be perfect. I knew that wasn't realistic, and that her name had nothing to do with it. But then I discovered that there actually IS something to being Literal. Because my dad's favorite expression is "trouble in paradise." And that's EXACTLY what I've found in Ms. Paradise's fifth-grade class.

This is disappointing, because over the summer, I was *really* excited for fifth grade in general. I'm usually scared about a new school year (or about anything new, really) because what if it's terrible and everyone hates me? But this year, for the first time in all of elementary school, I *knew* I was ready for it. Because what can go wrong when you're the oldest kids in school?

On the first morning back, everything felt so familiar. I walked down the hallways I knew so well and waved hello to all my old teachers. I saw younger kids looking nervous as they walked in to their new classrooms, and I wanted to say, "Don't worry, you're going to have the BEST time with Ms. Bloom!" or "It's okay, Mr. Flight's leaf project is hard work, but it's worth it!"

When I walked into Ms. Paradise's class, I was ready to take on fifth grade. I was sure this would be the best year EVER.

So it was a bit of a letdown when I realized that Ms. Paradise is what my mom would call "A Bit Much."

Ms. Paradise is new to our school this year, and came from teaching third graders. She's big on following rules, and doing exercises and worksheets, which doesn't leave much room for creativity (though her big fluffy dresses with flowers all over them ARE very creative, so at least there's that). And whenever she talks to you one-on-one, her voice gets very high and syrupy, even though it definitely doesn't sound that way when she talks to adults.

Ms. Paradise covers the walls of our classroom with neon paper cutouts of pineapples, which are VERY bright and distracting. They're also kind of a strange choice (I love food as much as the next person, but if I had to pick a class Theme, I'd at least pick food with a little more variety, like sandwiches).

Plus she put me in the blue reading group, not the purple (which is the highest), because she says my reading comprehension needs some work when it comes to grammar.

Which is ridiculous.

In case you hadn't noticed, I'm not the biggest fan of Ms. Paradise. My mom keeps saying things like "Give her a chance," and "Cilla, you've only been in school for a month!" But I'd argue that when you're faced with the kind of person who says "My, it's roasty toasty back here!" when the classroom fans aren't working, you're probably never going to get along.

Worst of all, on that first day, instead of talking about all the exciting fifth-grade things we'd be doing in the year ahead, Ms. Paradise began talking about middle school. Specifically, how much we need to do to get ready for it.

I don't think I'm "being bad with change" (which is what my mom says I am) for wanting to enjoy fifth grade. Also, for not wanting to talk about middle school ever, and possibly maybe never going. I'm not looking forward to when the middle schoolers come to visit our class later this year to tell us about it, or any of the other middle school–related things Ms. Paradise keeps talking about.

In fact, I wish we could just enjoy elementary school, because there's SO MUCH to love. Fifth grade has so many exciting parts—like field trips, and science projects, and *band*, which is a special fifth-grade elective. This summer, I started playing the TUBA, which is big, Dramatic, and VERY loud, which means it's probably the best instrument ever. Mr. Kendall, our music teacher, says I'm a "very strong player" (even if all I can play so far are scales and "Twinkle Twinkle, Little Star"). And I love the tuba so much that when Ms. Paradise had us do beginning-of-the-year introduction cards with facts about ourselves, after "writer," "great older sister," and "cheese connoisseur," I put "Tuba Player."

So everyone would know.

And I don't know why Ms. Paradise feels like she has to mention middle school every day, when there are things like band to focus on instead. In fact, sometimes I wonder if she's a Trickster Figure trying to distract us from the REAL Adventure, which is fifth grade. (Tricksters come up a lot in Quests, and you have to watch out for them, and possibly solve riddles to get away.) And sometimes I pretend that my tuba is a Magical Talisman that can help me resist her and protect me from the worried feelings I get whenever she mentions next year.

But the tuba can only do so much. So even though I've been trying hard to like Ms. Paradise, it's been a whole month and things are only getting worse. Especially since Ms. Paradise has started to talk about things like "middle school Expectations." And I'm sorry to say that she's ESPECIALLY big on these Expectations, and what counts as middle school material, when it comes to writing.

I learned this last week, which is also when I realized just how many Struggles I had to overcome before fifth grade was over.

It happened like this:

We were doing a writing unit, and even though I still wasn't sure how I felt about Ms. Paradise, I was excited to show her my stories.

Ms. Paradise wanted us to follow a worksheet that was all about how stories are like watermelons and ideas like seeds (which was a nice Simile, which is a Literary way of saying comparison). Ms. Paradise said that instead of telling the whole watermelon, you start with a seed. So instead of "I went to an amusement park and ate ice cream, rode some rides, and had a great day and came home," you start with a tiny part of that. Like "The ice cream dripped from the cone down on my hands and was sticky and delicious." That way, you start with details, and it's easier for the reader to imagine your story, and they'll want to know more and keep reading.

The assignment seemed fun. I love specifics and details, and since stories are my life's work, I felt good about the examples I'd picked (plus I didn't even say anything about how surprised I was about the whole watermelon Theme, given Ms. Paradise's obsession with pineapples).

My story began:

On Zebulon 5, a prophecy was known. That
one day a hero would save the planet from
its endless war, a hero who would fly on
feathers of steel.
   But the people of Zebulon 5 didn't
believe the prophecy. They laughed and
said it was a Silly story.
   And so did Tilly the baker's daughter.
   Until one day, she woke up, and she had
grown silver, metal *wings*.

I thought this was a *great* start. I didn't start with Tilly growing wings—I started with the seed of the prophecy. I knew this beginning was perfect for drawing a reader in. They wouldn't be able to resist asking how it ends, and where the wings came from, and when Tilly will discover that she can also shoot golden light out of her hands and use it to bring her world to peace (Spoiler Alert). I was sure I'd done a good job.

Only apparently my story wasn't what Ms. Paradise had in mind.

"Um," she said, her voice chirpy, "this is certainly interesting."

"Thank you," I said (because interesting is a good thing to be).

"But why don't you write about something a little more relatable?" she went on. "Remember, next year you're going to have teachers with high expectations of your writing—middle school expectations. They're going to want your work to make your readers feel *real* emotion. So be a bit more serious, okay?"

Ms. Paradise said all of this with a smile, like she was just trying to help. Then she walked away with her big sleeves bouncing as she went.

I was frustrated because, this IS Serious. We're talking the fate of Zebulon 5.

And if you don't feel real emotion when you hear that an entire planet might be torn apart by galactic war, then I can't help you.

For the rest of the activity, I sat and looked at my story and tried to figure out where it could be more Serious and why it didn't meet middle school Expectations.

It didn't help how I was feeling when Ms. Paradise asked Mimi Donnelly to read her story out loud as an "excellent and strong example." Mimi also wants to be a writer (and yes, fair, writing is the best career you could ever choose but, also, couldn't Mimi want to do something else?). And as she read, I didn't understand why her story—which was one whole page about reaching out to touch a doorknob, and the feeling of turning it—WAS right for middle school. Even though it had some nice descriptions, who wants to read a story all about reaching for a doorknob without actually opening the door and seeing what's behind it?

But luckily, I have my friends, who are all in Ms. Paradise's class with me.

"Zebulon Five sounds so cool," Colleen said.

"I want wings," Melissa said. "Will you tell us the story at recess?"

"Will there be explosions?" Alien-Face McGee asked.

I appreciated all of their support, and the

answer to both of these questions was, of course, "Yes!"

There was plenty of time to tell Tilly's story at recess. Now that we're in fifth grade, there's less playing or making up games, and more sitting and talking. For the most part I really like this new way of being together. We tell stories and make jokes, and sometimes Melissa brings in paper and teaches us origami, because she's taking a class at her library. Usually, Colleen, Melissa, and I like to sit on the swings, and Mimi Donnelly and her friends sit on the tire swings or sometimes the picnic benches, and a group of kids from Mr. Mason's class have claimed the climbing structure.

But we still run around too. Sometimes we play tag, and other times Colleen and Melissa kick a soccer ball around the field and I'm their Coach. (This is VERY fun. Even though I don't know anything about soccer or sports of any kind, I'm great at saying Dramatic things like "This is everything you've trained for!" and "You can do it; you were born for this!"). And this way I can help Colleen and Melissa improve their Muscle Memory, which is how you teach your body to remember things even faster than your brain, and Colleen says it will help them win the championship this year, which is an exciting idea.

Alien-Face McGee doesn't spend that much time with us at recess now that we're in fifth grade, which is too bad. But he runs by a lot with the other boys he plays with, and he always waves when he passes us, so that's nice. And if Melissa and Colleen are playing a kickball game, he'll usually leave his game and keep me company cheering for them.

That day at recess, I told Colleen, Melissa, and Alien-Face more about Zebulon 5, and after Alien-Face went to go play with the other boys,

Melissa told us her story, which was about a talking watermelon seed (which is a Literalness that I support).

We were talking and joking and coming up with names for her watermelon seed, and ideas for how Tilly would get around (when she's not flying, she rides a jet-black motorcycle), when Tim #2 came by like he does every day now, to say, "Hi, Colleen!" Then he just stood there. And after a little too long he said, "Oh, um, hi, Melissa. Hi, Cilla." And then he ran away.

This is another funny fifth-grade change. It just seems to keep happening. Tim #2 and Melvin and Shelby all walk by at least once every recess to say, "Hi, Colleen!" I'm not sure why they do, or why Colleen always trips or knocks things over when Melvin's around, or why Alien-Face blushes and giggles when Tim #1 smiles at him.

But it's no big deal. We all still have a great time (and it's also kind of funny), so I don't think much about it. Plus Melissa also doesn't quite get it either, so when it happens, we smile at each other and giggle (but nicely).

On this particular day, Melvin ran over right behind Tim #2, so Colleen got up to talk to him. Melissa hopped down from her swing to talk to them too, and I decided I'd stay and keep swinging and wait for them to be done. I was imagining what it would feel like to be actually flying, just like Tilly, when I heard a voice from the tire swings where Mimi Donnelly and her friends had been sitting and, I realized, had overheard my story.

"Well, you make up Silly stories too, right, Mimi?" her friend Lisa said in a teasing voice.

"No way." The familiar voice of Mimi Donnelly was loud and made it very clear that these "Silly" stories were bad things. "*My* stories are grown-up," she said. "They're not about made-up things like people growing wings. That's immature."

"Yeah," Lisa said. "What a baby."

My feet scraped the wood-chip-covered ground. Without meaning to, I'd stopped swinging, and my swing came to a stop with a small squeak.

Mimi turned and saw me.

Her face got red.

But then Lisa giggled, a not-very-nice giggle. And Mimi went *on*.

"No offense," she said, shrugging like it was no big deal. "But . . . you should really stop telling stories like that when you get to middle school. My sister's there now, and she says no one in middle school would *ever* talk that way."

Lisa and Mimi's other friends giggled some more.

"Yeah," Lisa added. "But you're the girl who always talks about the tuba, right? I don't know why you play it. It's a boy instrument. Right, Mimi?"

"Well . . ." Mimi looked at Lisa, then back at me. "I guess," she said, the redness staying in her cheeks. "I mean, all the other girls play the flute, or clarinet, or sometimes the saxophone," she added.

"Yeah." Lisa nodded.

I didn't know what to say.

I wanted to tell them that my story wasn't Silly—it was a good one (which I know because of the whole Literary Greatness thing). And the tuba was AMAZING, and she was just jealous because she wasn't playing it. Plus I wanted to tell Mimi Donnelly and Lisa and everyone on the tire swing that they were NOT very nice.

There were so many other things I could have said too, like, "Well, your sister in middle school sounds kind of boring," or "Maybe no one in middle school would read a story about doorknobs either."

But I couldn't find the words. And Colleen and Melissa were standing over with Melvin and hadn't heard, so I didn't have any friends to be on my side.

So I just said, "Oh."

The whistle blew, telling us that there were ten minutes left in recess, and I'd never been happier to hear it. I jumped up from the swing and walked away, trying not to imagine how Mimi and her friends were probably watching me go and giggling.

Out of the corner of my eye I saw Colleen wave, and I knew she thought everything was fine. So I gave a small wave back and headed into the school building for what's usually my favorite time of the day.

Because in fifth grade, during the last ten minutes of recess, we have Library Privileges.

"Cilla!" Ms. Clutter called as I walked in.

"Hi, Ms. Clutter," I said, smiling in spite of Mimi Donnelly.

Ms. Clutter is our school librarian. She came to our school last year in fourth grade, and she's been one of my favorite people ever since. Ms. Clutter knows EVERYTHING about books and stories. She always has a good book to recommend, and we both LOVE Adventures and Selena Moon and the Jenny Ojukwo: Pirate Queen series. Ms. Clutter also has the BEST style ever. That afternoon, she wore a purple dress with a silver belt and matching silver glasses. She always wears a scarf over her hair, and that day it was covered in a pattern of swirling *galaxies* that flowed around her head and down her back and fluttered behind her like a cape. This is also, incidentally, why I sometimes make up stories that Ms. Clutter is really a superhero. Because you can't be that great, and know so much about books and libraries, and just be a normal person, now can you?

I go to the library almost every day. Sometimes it's to get a new book. Sometimes, if I'm still in the middle of a book, it's just to say hi to Ms. Clutter and to tell her about the story so far. Ms. Clutter is always really interested in what I'm reading, and she loves it when I act out the books, and she'll always talk about parts that I don't understand or didn't like.

That day, I told Ms. Clutter my Zebulon 5 story, which she LOVED.

Then she suggested other science fiction books she thought I'd enjoy. She said they were some of her favorite books too.

So I felt better. And when she handed me a book with a winged centaur on the cover flying over a rainbow planet, I suddenly found myself asking, "Do you think this is a middle school–kind of story, Ms. Clutter?"

"Oh, absolutely," she said. "This book is *very* popular up at the middle school."

"Really?" I said. "WOW. So it's a Serious story?"

"Yes," she said. "Absolutely. It's all about good triumphing over evil, and serious questions about how to stand up for what you know is right. It's a real epic," she said with a smile. "You might find some great inspiration there."

"An Epic," I whispered, looking down at the book in my hands.

And that's how I knew.

In Adventures, heroes always have a Wise Guide who tells them what their Quest is, or how to start their Adventure, or that with power comes responsibility. Ms. Stauffer, my fourth-grade teacher, taught me this.

So I'm guessing Ms. Clutter is mine.

That day, I knew I had a problem, and a lot of

Struggles to overcome. Because even though Mimi Donnelly and her friends are mean, and I know I shouldn't listen to them, Mimi does have a sister in middle school. And even if Ms. Paradise is A Bit Much, she's also a teacher, and she does know what middle school is like.

And if Ms. Paradise AND Mimi are saying I'm not ready for middle school, maybe it's actually true. What if I'm *not* grown-up enough or mature enough for middle school?

Most people would despair in the face of these Struggles.

But Ms. Clutter helped me find the answer.

That day, I left the library filled with purpose, ready to begin my Quest.

I knew I had to write an Epic, a story that was about Serious questions, a story that would end in triumph, a story that would show everyone— especially Mimi Donnelly—how grown-up I am.

And no amount of trouble in paradise (or on Zebulon 5) can stop me.

2

FOURTH GRADE AND FAMILY: A YEAR IN HAIKU

Last year, in fourth grade, we studied poetry.
I LOVE poetry, because it's all about using words
to get at the heart of what you want to say. Ms.
Stauffer said good poetry "captures the essence,"
which means poems are about the most important
parts of a person or thing. And I think the best
way to do this is through my favorite kind of poem:
haikus.

Haikus are really short poems that have a certain
number of syllables in each line (five in the first
line, seven in the second, and five again in the third),
which makes it like a puzzle to put them together.
For example:

Things change, time passes.
I'm still destined for greatness,
though. What a relief!

Or:

He may be funny,
but Alien-Face McGee
is annoying too.

Or:

She tells the best jokes,
She is so Silly and fun,
Melissa, a star.

I'm really proud of this one because it really DOES get at the essence of things, because Melissa is actually very quiet most of the time (which I can definitely relate to). And it's only when you get to know her that you realize how funny and Silly she can be, so this poem captures something not many people get to see.

I also wrote a poem for Colleen, which goes:

She's brave and strong, a
whirlwind on the soccer field.
My best friend, Colleen.

This poem got extra points from Ms. Stauffer because it has a Metaphor, which is when you use another object to describe something else, without saying "like" or "as." I'm very proud of it because it REALLY gets at Colleen's essence. She's isn't afraid to give class presentations, or say what she thinks, or even, as I've mentioned, to go to middle school. And she's AMAZING at soccer, and I really like watching her games.

Colleen also got SUPER tall in fourth grade. I can't wait to catch up with her, which I know will happen soon because my mom keeps saying that these are years of big and unexpected Changes.

And getting taller is a BIG change. I'm excited, even if my mom does get weird when we talk about Changes and her voice gets funny and she says, "If you ever want to talk, I'm always here." Which is nice, but I don't know why she thinks I'll need to talk about it. If anything, growing will make things easier, since I'll finally be able to reach our top kitchen shelves.

In an Epic, Colleen, Melissa, and Alien-Face would be my Allies and Brave Companions (who are the friends who fight courageously by your side, and sometimes include elves, gnomes, or talking animals). I'm lucky to have so many Companions and friends, especially in the face of Foes like Mimi and Lisa.

And that's not even all. I have a big family too, filled with Companions and Wise Guides and other kinds of Allies. In fact, last year it got even BIGGER.

The change in my family can be described like this:

New babies are loud.

Alas, I just want to sleep.

I still like her, though.

Because last winter, I got *another* little sister. Her name is Esther Lee-Jenkins, though we mostly call her Essie.

Essie ♡

Big eyes that watch EVERYTHING

Hair that sticks up no matter how much you brush it

Always trying to pull herself up on something and hold it so she can stand, draw on walls, or both

Baby crayon that she's always trying to use or eat

When my first little sister, Gwendolyn, was born, I was NOT happy. You might remember this, because I possibly wrote a book about how not happy I was. But once Gwendolyn came, I realized that I like having her around. In fact, she's pretty great.

Gwen!

She's MUCH bigger (two years old!)

And she can talk (and does it A LOT)

lots of hair that I braided

Batman with a tutu (Gwen's favorite toy: they're dance legends together. Also, I added the tutu – it didn't come with Batman, but it should.)

When I heard that I was getting another new sister, I wondered if I'd be upset or nervous again. But adding Essie to our family has actually been much easier than I'd expected. When she was born, I knew just what to do. I knew how to hold her, and how to feed her, and how to put my fingers in my ears so the crying wouldn't be so loud. Plus it was fun to teach Gwendolyn these things, and to help her be an older sister, too.

Having two younger sisters is also convenient because every Epic Adventure needs some Comic Relief, no matter how Serious it is. And TRUST ME, they are *excellent* at this, plus the funny things they do are great inspiration for poems. Like:

Gwendolyn is fun,
Gwendolyn is nice,
Gwendolyn spilled all my juice to chew upon the ice.

Gwendolyn is sweet,
Gwendolyn is quick,
Gwendolyn ate all my candy, that's why she was sick.

This is an example of a nonfiction poem, by the way, which means it's true. And Gwendolyn really does want the ice in your glass because she likes to chew on it, and she'll knock over your cup to get it. And let's not speak about the Great Cilla-Left-Her-Bag-of-Halloween-Candy-on-the-Floor-Where-Gwen-Could-Get-It Disaster of Fourth Grade.

Gwen and Essie are also going to be an important part of my Epic, I've decided recently. Because I want everyone to know how grown-up I am, and they are just the way to do it.

I call my plan: Operation Babysitting.

Operation Babysitting is perfect because Babysitting is all about being responsible, and not only for yourself but for other people too. So once I'm a Babysitter, everyone in fifth grade (and then middle school) will know just how Grown-up and Serious I am. Plus, Babysitting also means you get money, which is important if you want to go to the movies or get ice cream with your friends by yourself (not that we're allowed to do this yet, but it's a BIG part of being grown-up, and we're working on it).

Best of all, I *knew* my parents would say yes, because my dad has a new job and works from home now, which means he's on the phone ALL THE TIME. Things are *really* busy, and my mom and dad have less time to do things like go out and have dinner together. So when I told them my plan today, I smiled and waited for them to say, "Wow, thank you so much. What a fabulous (and grown-up) offer, Cilla!"

Unfortunately, though, that's not quite how it happened.

In fact, they said "no." And then, "Maybe in a few years."

These people.

Good thing I'm persistent. I KNOW I can change their minds. So instead of arguing (too much), I went to go sit and play with Gwen and Essie, to show my parents just how great I am at being an older sister.

Essie is eight months old, which means she can sit up, and she can wiggle around EVERYWHERE by pulling herself on her stomach. She has a lot of hair (which is an Injustice if I ever heard one, since I was bald when I was a baby).

But at least it's fun, because her hair sticks straight up, and no amount of hair gel or water can make it lie flat. Also, cutting it makes it MUCH worse. My dad and I learned this the other day, when he said, "Don't worry, Ellen, I'll just trim an inch—it'll fix the whole problem!" He was wrong, and now it looks like Essie has a permanent mohawk, and my mom laughed until she cried when she saw it, and so did I.

My sisters have their own Epic Destinies too, which I've helped them find, because I'm a great Big Sister that way. Gwen's took a while to discover (a whole book in fact!). But now we know that she's a future dance legend. And it's DEFINITELY true because she NEVER stops moving and knocking things over, which, as I try to explain to my parents, just can't be helped: You can't fight Fate.

Essie's Destiny, though, was much easier to find.

In fact, we discovered her Destiny of greatness the day she tried her first bite of baby food. She took one bite of her mashed squash, smiled, grabbed the spoon from my hand, and drew a PICTURE with it. Specifically, what my art teacher (who should be our music teacher) Ms. Song would call abstract art.

Then she grabbed a Cheerio while I was trying to get the spoon back, crushed it, and sprinkled it on her masterpiece.

I knew, then and there, that she is a future painting prodigy (and "prodigy" is a fancy word for "legend" or "extraordinaire" that I learned in Ms. Stauffer's fourth-grade class).

Gwen has changed a lot since my last book too:

She's a toddler now, so she walks, talks, and says funny things. She wasn't so sure about Essie when she first came along (which I can relate to). But I'm teaching her to be a great Big Sister (and making sure my parents notice what a good job I'm doing).

For example, my mom's been a little worried recently, because Essie doesn't really talk.

I think it's because she's too busy watching the world and taking in the sights and feelings to put in her art.

But my mom says it's because there are so many people to talk for her (which doesn't make sense, because, yes, we are good talkers, but shouldn't that mean that we set a good example for her and she sees how to do it?).

But, in case my mom IS right, I'm trying to help by asking her more questions so she gets used to the idea of talking. Like tonight, when my mom asked, "Essie, do you want the mashed peas or squash?"

"Peas," Gwen said.

"Well, maybe," my mom said. "Let's see. Peas or squash, Essie?"

"But peas are her favorite," Gwen said.

My mom sighed. "Okay, but, Essie—"

Just then, Essie reached for the jar of peas (because Gwen was right—we all know she likes peas best).

My mom threw up her hands and then opened the jar of peas.

So I thought I'd help and ask another question, since they're so important.

"Essie," I asked, "do you want apple juice or water?

"She likes apple juice," Gwen answered.

And even though Gwen wasn't supposed to say anything, it *was* the right answer, and I wanted to support her (like a good Big Sister—and Babysitter—should).

"Very good, Gwen!" I said, turning to her, beaming. "High five!"

So we did.

I was glad my parents could see me being so responsible. And Essie was happy, which I knew because she drank her juice and then painted with the peas, and smiled and made happy giggling noises when I told her it was a "masterpiece."

So score one for Operation Babysitting.

I had a *little* setback after dinner, though, when I said I'd put Gwen to bed by myself, to show that I could.

It went something like this:

Me: Let's go to bed, Gwen!

Gwen: No!

Me: But, Gwen, you love bedtime.

Gwen: NO. I HATE bedtime! (Hate is a big Theme with Gwen lately.)

Me: But look at your pajamas, Gwen. Aren't they pretty?

Gwen: NO! (No is another big Theme with Gwen, too.)

Me: Come on, Gwen, just one foot?

Gwen: NO.

Me: Please?

Gwen: [Cries]

Me: Don't cry! Here, have a truck! Vroom vroom!

Gwen: [Stops crying] Can the truck fly?

Me: Of course. I mean, it is a magic truck after all. And you know, it doesn't just fly. It also can turn invisible, and . . .

[Twenty minutes later]

Mom: Young Lady, what is going on here? And look at this mess! Gwen is supposed to be in bed!

Me: Oops.

Gwen: Bed?! I LOVE bedtime!

Me: Sigh.

End scene.

But I will say it was a good story we made up. And later, while I was cleaning up the BIG mess we'd made, and my mom was putting Gwen to bed, I wrote a new haiku.

It goes:

I, Babysitter
So grown-up. Be impressed and
then give me money.

Which I think gets nicely at the essence of the issue.

SYNONYMS ARE SERIOUS BUSINESS

A Synonym is a word that means the same thing as another. So, for example, you could say Gwen's dances are "funny" or "amusing" (or "destructive" or "make a huge mess around the house"), depending on how you look at it.

We're learning about Synonyms in school. I love this unit, because Synonyms are all about giving you new ways to say things and new ways to see them. So if something's really important, you can say it in lots of different ways, like "I am destined for greatness," and also "fated for celebrity," plus "on the road to fame."

Synonyms can also add new meanings to your

words. So I could say, "Dad's new job means he's busy." But I could also use a Synonym and say, "Dad's new job means he's overloaded" or "buried under work" or "a mess" (which all are Synonyms for the same idea, but each with an added layer of chaos).

There's even a special book called a thesaurus, which has lists and lists of Synonyms. Which is great to know, because words are always excellent to learn.

Or at least, that's how things should be.

But ever since Mimi Donnelly, it's like I haven't been able to stop looking for new Synonyms. Less-great Synonyms.

So if I want to tell a fun story at recess, I wonder if another Synonym for fun is maybe "Silly." Or "Immature." And sometimes, I don't end up telling my story, after all, because I'm not quite sure how to tell the difference.

Now that I know to listen for these Synonyms too, I'm realizing that they're EVERYWHERE. In fact, when you know what to listen for, it's hard to be on the playground without overhearing conversations that seem to have them. Like:

"Middle school is going to be the best because there won't be all this little-kid stuff, they don't even have swings there." (Phoebe.)

Or:

"My mom tutors eighth graders and they all look *super* grown-up, not like any of the kids here." (Leah.)

Or:

"I don't know why my parents can't let me be more Independent. They don't believe I can handle things on my own, but I CAN, I know it." (Colleen.)

And every time I hear these things I worry a little, because I'm not always sure what's Independence, and if I'm doing it right, and if I'll be Immature if I don't do things on my own. Which is why I haven't really told Colleen or my parents about Mimi and her friend Lisa. But that at least works out, because heroes usually work alone, especially when it comes to the big Epic showdown. So I know my Independence will really pay off.

It's also been harder to enjoy band. In fact, I haven't practiced much at all in the last week. Mr. Kendall keeps saying things like, "Come on, Cilla, you should know this song by now," and my mom and dad keep saying things like, "Cilla, what's up? You love practicing."

Which is true. But my tuba has changed since that day with Mimi. It doesn't seem like a Magical Talisman anymore, which is supposed to make you feel good and safe and protected. Now when I'm in band, instead of enjoying the feeling of puffing out my cheeks and hearing how all the different sounds come together in a song, I'm wondering what other people are thinking. I wonder if they think I'm weird. Or if they're asking themselves why I'm here, in the brass section. And most of all, I'm wondering about Synonyms.

Because I hadn't known that "girl" is a Synonym for "not allowed to play the tuba."

Today, this was bugging me more than usual. Because OF COURSE Mimi Donnelly and Lisa play the flute. And just before we started practice,

Lisa leaned over and whispered something to Mimi. They looked back toward me and giggled.

I thought about asking Colleen about the tuba at recess, because Colleen is in band too and plays the oboe. But apparently there was an Emergency Yearbook Meeting. And Melissa isn't in band, so she doesn't really know how it works. So when I asked, "Do you think it's weird that I play the tuba?" she just said, "No, I think it's great! Why?"

"No reason," I said with a little sigh.

"Well," Melissa said, looking at me like she was trying figure out a puzzle, or take a temperature, "do you want to do origami?"

"I guess," I said, trying to sound more excited than I felt (I usually LOVE origami and Melissa is a GREAT teacher, and it was nothing against it or her. I just wasn't in an origami kind of mood).

"Okay. Or . . . ," she went on, "I was just reading a book about these girls who find fairies outside and leave them food and make houses for them during the day to come live in at night. I thought it would be a fun game."

"YES," I said. "And we could use leaves for roofs and acorns for cups and bowls."

"YES," she said. We were both grinning. "Let's grab some supplies, there's a pile of leaves by the swings!"

"Okay," I said. "Only . . ." I glanced over at the swings. Mimi was there with her friends.

"Only, why don't we go play in the field?" I asked, gesturing the other way, where there were less leaves but a lot more grass and empty space and not-Mimis-and-Lisas. "There's more stuff out there."

"Okay!" Melissa said.

And we ran off to build houses out of sticks and grass, far away from everyone else, where no one could hear our stories or think we were Silly or come up with more Synonyms to tell us what we could or couldn't do.

This afternoon, Ye Ye picked me up from school.

"I thought we could have a special afternoon together," he said, "in Chinatown."

"Yes!" I said. Because Chinatown is one of my favorite, treasured, cherished places on earth. (All Synonyms that mean it's GREAT.)

"I just have to drop something off at the community center," he said. "So we'll swing by there first."

The community center is a small brick building, right next to a highway at the edge of Chinatown. But inside, you'd never know that the road was so close. Inside, all you can hear are the sounds of people talking and laughing, sometimes in English but mostly in Chinese.

We walked in, and everyone said, "Hello, hello!" when they saw us, because EVERYONE knows Ye Ye. In fact, just walking down the hallway took a while because so many people said hi and asked questions and sometimes in between the Chinese I heard things like, "Tutoring tomorrow?" And Ye Ye saying things like, "Of course!" and "Did the new books come in for the reading room?" and "Ay yah,

Mrs. Cheung fell? Give me her phone number, I'll go sit with her this weekend."

We waved goodbye as we left, and I promised to come back and visit again soon. Then, together, we turned away from the highway, into Chinatown, and walked to our favorite dumpling restaurant for a soup dumpling snack, laughing and talking all the way.

Soup dumplings come in big woven baskets. They're thick, chewy dumplings filled with hot, delicious soup broth. To eat them you bite off the tops, being careful so you won't spill the soup inside. Then you slurp out the broth, balancing your dumpling on a wide, flat spoon. I'm VERY good at this, though when one of my dumplings burst as I tried to pick it up with my chopsticks (which is always Tragic because then the soup inside spills out), Ye Ye took it instead and gave me his unbroken one, which is probably the nicest thing anyone's ever done for me.

And except when we were slurping our dumplings, there were no quiet moments at all, because

Ye Ye and I always have SO MANY things to talk about. I told him all about Melissa and the fairies and how INCREDIBLE the yearbook's going to be because Colleen is working on it. (Though I didn't tell him about the tuba. In fact, when he asked about it I said, "I don't care about the tuba anymore, it's just not for me." His forehead wrinkled when I said this, and he looked at me funny. But he saw that I didn't want to talk about it, so he didn't ask anything else. Which was nice of him.)

All around us were SO MANY people who knew Ye Ye, and even the waiters waved and came over to say hello.

"Do you come to Chinatown every day?" I asked, between dumpling bites.

"Most days," he said. "Since I retired."

"And you help people, and do things for the community center?"

"Mmmhmm." He nodded as he slurped a dumpling.

"Why?" I asked.

"Well," he said, laying down his spoon and

chopsticks to rest on his plate, "when I first came to America, I was all by myself. I didn't know anyone. That's very lonely. But then I found Chinatown. They took me in, and taught me to get around, and invited me into their homes. They were like my family. Auntie Linda's mom even helped me get new clothes for a college dance, because I didn't know what to wear."

"Really?!" I said, giggling a little at the idea of Ye Ye trying to get fancy for a dance. "That was so nice of them."

"Yes," he said with a happy, remembering kind of smile. "So, now that I can, I volunteer. I tutor English, or I give advice to students who are here on their own, like I was. Or I just talk with them, so they won't be lonely. And sometimes I visit people around Chinatown if they're home sick, or just need company."

"Wow, Ye Ye," I said.

I knew he spent a lot of time in Chinatown. But I had NO idea he did all of this. And I'd never heard about these feelings from when he was younger.

"When you were lonely," I asked, "was it because you were the only one? I mean, the only student from China?"

"Yes," he said. "There were a few others, but not many. And American students sometimes wouldn't talk with us, and made fun of us."

"NO," I gasped.

"Unfortunately, yes," he said. "They thought we shouldn't be there."

"But . . . you were a student too!" I said, feeling my cheeks get hot because that was a long time ago but it wasn't fair *at all*. And suddenly, all these feelings were pouring out. "What did you do?" I asked. "And how do you make people see that you're *supposed* to be there? And what if they *always* think you don't belong, and that you're not mature or Serious, or, I mean . . ." I trailed off, frustrated.

Ye Ye reached across the table and took my hand.

"You know, Cilla," he said slowly, "there will always be people like this. But when I was young, I just decided to live my life and ignore them. When people do this, it's because of *them*. Maybe they're ignorant, or scared of something, or they're just not happy with themselves. All you can do is keep on going and remember—it's *their* problem. Not yours."

"Oh," I said.

We were quiet for a few minutes after that, but that was okay, because there were more soup dumplings to slurp. Which is a nice way to spend time when you're also thinking.

"Do you have homework for today?" Ye Ye asked.

"A little," I said. "Actually, there's this marching song we learned in band today that I should practice. You'll love it too—can I play it for you at home?"

"Perfect." Ye Ye smiled. "I can't wait."

It was a beautiful day as we left Chinatown. So we walked and enjoyed the clear sky and the fall leaves crunching around us. As we rounded a corner, talking and laughing, I suddenly saw something that made me gasp.

It was a BEAUTIFUL carousel, all carved in wood and painted in bright colors.

"Wow," I said, just as he said, "Wah," because it had the most beautiful animals, not just horses, but also foxes, and rabbits, and whales, and butterflies. I looked at my Ye Ye and grinned, and he looked at me and grinned, and we understood each other *perfectly*.

I rode a giant turtle, a hawk, and an owl. And on each new ride, Ye Ye made a big show of getting up on an animal in one big jump, which made me laugh and clap because it was *really* impressive. He rode a lobster (which was very funny, and we made lobster-pincer shapes with our hands while he did), a butterfly, and a fox.

It was the BEST carousel I've ever been on, and we both wanted to stay. I sort of hoped we'd be able to ride every single animal (except maybe the squirrel, because there's something about the idea of a squirrel that's bigger than me that I don't like).

But Ye Ye looked at his watch and said, "Ay yah, your Nai Nai will worry if we don't get home. Not to mention the tuba!"

But before we left we took one last ride, me on a rabbit, him on a GIANT grasshopper. We skipped away from the carousel together, and I didn't care who saw, because yes it was Silly and maybe not mature but it was SO MUCH FUN. On the ride home, we named our animals and imagined what the animals would do if they came to life at night and fought crime (which I've decided definitely happens). Then I gave a tuba concert for Nai Nai and Ye Ye at home, and they clapped, and Gwen danced, and Essie kicked to the beat.

The day had gone round and round, bad then good, up and down, and lots of other Synonyms for change.

I'd learned a lot. I'd learned about words, and band, and other things too.

And, most of all, that Ye Ye is very Wise. And quite possibly, the best Ye Ye in the world.

No other Synonyms required.

4

A NOT-SO-NORMAL DAY

Today started out normal.

And then it wasn't.

But I'm going to start with the normal, because that's what I wish the whole day had been.

Today I woke up with crushed Oreos in my hair that I somehow missed last night in the shower (normal).

I convinced my dad to pick out clothes for me so I could change under the comforter because it's COLD in the mornings now (normal).

I ate cereal for breakfast (normal).

I said no when Gwen wanted to eat my cereal because she's convinced that everything I have is better than what she has (normal).

I said, "Argh, Gwen!" when she plunked her hand into my cereal bowl and grabbed some cereal anyway (normal).

I wiped splashed milk out of my hair while Dad took Gwen away crying, and my mom helped me and said "Ew" (normal).

I caught the bus and sat with Colleen, like I always do, and we talked about how the yearbook committee is looking for the right cover and hasn't found anything yet. She's worried that they'll go with something boring and the yearbook won't be perfect. I told her that it *would* be perfect, because she's working on it, and then I told her a joke that made her smile. (Normal.)

In class we practiced Synonyms (normal), and when Ms. Paradise asked, "Who can think of a Synonym for 'good'?" she called on me, and I was SO EXCITED to tell everyone and said, "Supercalifragilisticexpialidocious!"

But Ms. Paradise said, "No, that's not a real word." Then she called on Mimi Donnelly, who said, "'Excellent' is a Synonym for 'good.'"

"Perfect, Mimi!" Ms. Paradise said with a big smile. And this was all, I'm sad to say, very normal.

In band, Lisa looked at me and giggled. "Her problem, not mine," I repeated to myself. "Her problem, not mine." But I still "accidentally" blew in my tuba right next to her ear when she passed by the tubas to go to the bathroom (which was also her problem, not mine, plus REALLY satisfying). And this, also, is normal.

At recess, Melissa taught me and Colleen to fold paper cranes, and Tim #2 and Melvin came over to say hello, and Alien-Face ran by and said,

"Silly Lee!" I shook my head and pretend-sighed and was pretend-mad, even though it makes me laugh because it's a joke we've had for a long time (plus he's always been annoying, so why stop now?).

I left recess when Mr. McKinstry blew his whistle for Library Privileges and found a new book all about a girl who's a brilliant scientist and uses her inventions to fly and turn herself invisible. I told Ms. Clutter all about the latest Jenny Ojukwo book and how much I liked it. And when I saw Mimi Donnelly in the library too, wandering near the Fantasy section, I grabbed the book I wanted quickly and hid it in front of me so she wouldn't see the cover and think I was Silly.

All of this, too, was normal.

And a pretty great day.

So I wasn't expecting it when I got home and found my mom there waiting for me on the front steps. She's usually at work when I get home, and my dad's the one who waits to pick me up from the bus now.

Her face was pale, and her eyes were red, like she had been crying.

"Everything's okay," was the first thing she said to me, hugging me tightly. "But something's happened. This morning, your Ye Ye had something called a stroke."

And just like that, normal was gone.

A stroke is not what it sounds like. It's not a stroke of luck, or a swimming stroke that takes you toward a finish line. A stroke, my mom explained, is when the blood that usually goes to our brains can't get there. It meant that some of the cells in Ye Ye's brain didn't have the oxygen they needed. And it happened while Nai Nai was out running errands, so it was a while before she came home and found him and could call an ambulance.

"But Ye Ye was so brave, and Nai Nai found him and knew exactly what to do. She leaped into action so fast," my mom said. "He's already awake. Your dad's at the hospital with him now. In a few days, we'll all go see him too."

"So . . . he'll be okay, right?" I asked. "He just has to get better, and then he'll be back to normal."

"Well," my mom said, "he'll absolutely be okay. But it might take a while. Strokes can be hard to recover from, and he might need to work for a long time, before he's on his feet again. The doctors will know more in the next few days. And you can visit him soon, maybe even tomorrow."

"Okay," I said quietly.

And I did feel better. Because this is my Ye Ye we're talking about. Ye Ye who is Wise and strong, and can pick me up, and twirl me around, and leap onto giant wooden grasshoppers.

So when my mom said she thought Ye Ye would really like a card from me, Gwendolyn, and Essie, I was excited to make it. I was in charge of it, which is smart, because Gwendolyn can't write, and even though Essie is destined for artistic fame, she hasn't really figured out that paper is for drawing, not eating.

I was glad to have something to do. After a few minutes of thinking, I knew *exactly* what to draw. I used bright colors, just like Ye Ye loves. And when I was done, I wrote all our names in big letters.

That night, when my dad came home, he looked tired. He sat down on the couch and said, "Come here, sweetie," and reached out his arm. So I went over and cuddled. I kept my face hidden in his shoulder, though, because I wanted to be grown-up, but I knew my face didn't look it.

He hugged me tight and said everything my mom had said—that Ye Ye was going to be okay, and Nai Nai was in the hospital with him, and we'd go visit this weekend.

But when I asked if that meant everything would be normal soon, he didn't really answer.

He gave me a hug good-night, but he didn't come in to sit with me and talk about books and say good night, like he normally does. Instead, he talked on the phone, pacing up and down the hall-way, talking first in Chinese to my Nai Nai, and then in English to my Auntie Eva, who lives in another city but is coming down this weekend to see Ye Ye.

And when I got up to go to the bathroom, I saw my mom and dad standing in the hallway, and my mom was hugging my dad, and he had his head on her shoulder, and she was rubbing his back and saying, "It's okay." And I realized that he was *crying*.

I tiptoed back to bed, and I lay there for a long, long time, before I fell asleep.

Today, after lots of phone calls with my Nai Nai, my dad said I could come visit in the hospital, though only for a few minutes. I told myself that it would be fine, and that there was nothing to worry about, and normal would come back the moment I saw him.

But something was different when we got to the hospital. At first, I couldn't figure out what. I've been in hospitals before—in fact, when Gwen was born, my mom had to stay there for a while. So I learned that hospitals can actually be nice places, with friendly people who make sure your mom is comfortable and smile when you walk by. When Essie was born and I had to go, I wasn't scared at all, and I was actually excited for the hospital trip, because it meant I could meet Essie and see my mom.

So I didn't think I'd be nervous when I went to see Ye Ye, and I held the flowers we'd gotten him very tightly. I'd picked the colors—red and yellow, like his favorite tie.

My dad knocked on a door, and we heard my Nai Nai say, "Come in."

The room was white and shiny. There was a curtain hung through the middle and another bed in the corner, with a stranger in it, behind the curtain. I saw my Nai Nai, giving me a tired smile from a chair by the wall. Auntie Eva was there next to her—she'd flown in late the night before. Usually, when I see her, I run to her, and she's always smiling and ready with a funny joke. But today she looked pale, with dark circles under her eyes.

And I didn't run to her right away.

I was too busy looking at the bed against the wall.

There, surrounded by metal stands and tubes and machines, was my Ye Ye.

Dad went to say hi to Ye Ye, with Gwen in one arm, and my mom took Essie to give Nai Nai and Auntie Eva a big hug. But I hung back, behind them. Because it *was* my Ye Ye. But it also seemed like it wasn't.

Ye Ye looked small, and more tired than I'd ever seen him. His face was white like paper, and there were needles in his arms. When he saw us and started to talk, only half of his mouth really moved, and only one of his eyes turned to look at me. Dad had warned me about this, but I hadn't expected his face to look so tired and droopy and different, or for him to seem so small in that big hospital bed with all those sharp things poking at him. He wore a strange white hospital gown that wasn't like the nice, colorful clothes that I know he loves.

Gwen had been fussing, but when she saw Ye Ye, she started to cry, and it wasn't just normal crying—she was *scared* of him.

"Come say hello, sweetie," my dad said, gesturing to me.

I took a deep breath and walked over.

"Hi, Ye Ye," I said quietly. "We brought you flowers."

Ye Ye reached out his hand, and I took it. He gave it a squeeze and said, "Thank you, Cilla," in a soft, slow way.

Which was different than the way he usually talks, but still nice.

I began to feel better.

I put the flowers on the windowsill and went to give Nai Nai a hug. Ye Ye gestured to the window and said something softly in Chinese.

"He says he loved the card, Cilla," my dad said. "See it there by the window?"

"Thanks," I said with a smile. "I'm so glad. Did you like the walrus I drew for you on the front?"

Ye Ye said something to my dad in Chinese. My dad answered, and Ye Ye spoke again.

"Yes," my dad said, turning to me. "He thought the colors were especially nice."

"Um, thanks." I looked back and forth, finally realizing what was bothering me. "B-but," I stammered, looking at Ye Ye, "why is Ye Ye telling you these things? Why isn't he talking to me?"

"Sweetie, let's let your mom say hello," my dad said. "Ye Ye needs to rest soon."

"Yes," Nai Nai said, patting my back in a way that was supposed to be soothing. "Very tired."

I didn't like this AT ALL.

My dad took me out into the hallway.

"But why was Ye Ye talking through you?" I asked again. I didn't want to, but I could feel my voice getting upset. "Why was he just talking in Chinese? Why didn't he talk to *me*?"

"Well, this is a new thing we're just learning," my dad said, kneeling down and taking my hand in his. "You see, when a brain is hurt, parts of it get cut off, and especially parts that have to do with language. Sometimes, when people have strokes, they can't talk at all. That's not what happened to Ye Ye. But, it seems like, right now, his brain can only handle one language, so he's gone back to his first one. Remember, he only learned English as a grown-up. And English is just too hard for him right now. He might get it back though. But for now, he's going to be speaking mostly Chinese."

"You mean . . ." I couldn't even find the words. "You mean," I said, trying again. "You mean, he can't talk to me anymore?"

"Of course he can," my dad said, pulling me into a hug. "It's just that English is going to be hard for him. And, sweetie, you should know that he's probably never going to be as fluent as he used to be. But there will always be someone there to help you translate, and he'll never stop being your Ye Ye. Even this morning—"

Just then, Nai Nai called my dad's Chinese name. "The doctor will be here soon," she said. "Can you help?"

"Of course, be right in," my dad said. "You okay, Cilla?" He put a hand on my shoulder. "I know it's hard, but it's going to be all right. Do you want to talk?"

I shook my head. So my dad just gave me a big, tight hug. And then my Nai Nai called again, and my dad went into the room.

I stood in the hallway, by myself, and watched the doctors and nurses walk by. Inside, I could hear the familiar sounds of my family—dad, Ye Ye, Auntie Eva, and Nai Nai, talking quietly in Chinese, Essie starting to fuss, and Gwendolyn asking for her Batman doll.

I thought about Ye Ye, and how he looked in that hospital bed. And I thought about the stories he always tells me, and the books he reads to me, and the Wisdom he knows. When I was little, I was scared of monsters in my closet, so he made up a story about unicorns fighting the monsters, and

it kept me safe. When I sometimes get mad at Gwendolyn, or jealous of her, Ye Ye always comes and sits with me, and we talk about my feelings. When Essie was born, Ye Ye taught me the songs he used to sing to his little cousin, and translated them into English for me. We made up a marching and singing game and paraded all over the house, singing in English and Chinese.

I remembered all these things, and I thought about what life would be like if he couldn't do them anymore.

What would happen if we couldn't tell stories, or talk, and how would he still be my Ye Ye, and how would I be his Cilla and granddaughter and—?

All of a sudden, it came to me.

NONE of this is normal. But I'm not going to let it stay this way.

I'm an Epic hero.

And Epics are all about overcoming the odds.

My dad says Ye Ye may never get his English back like it was before, but I know he will. Because I, Cilla Lee-Jenkins, future author extraordinaire, am going to teach it to him. And then he and I will ride victorious into the future. Into next year, and middle school, and a time when Ye Ye is back to being the one who teaches English and visits people who are lonely and can't leave the house. Not the other way around.

Back into the normal world. And the way everything is supposed to be.

IF THE PEN IS MIGHTIER THAN THE SWORD, THEN HOW COME I KEEP LOSING MY PEN?

I know everyone says the pen is mightier than the sword, but this has always seemed a little suspicious to me. I mean, I LOVE pens, and I absolutely think that stories are the best things in the world.

But no one brings a pen to slay a dragon—they bring a sword. Plus pens are just hard to keep track of, and heroes never lose their swords at the bottom of their backpacks, or forget them in their pants pockets and accidentally put them through the wash and make everything blue.

So I'm not sure if I completely believe in this whole pen-and-sword thing.

But, I can see how with Ye Ye, a pen is probably more helpful than a sword (even if a sword sounds more exciting).

So that's where I started when I visited Ye Ye in the hospital on the weekend.

My parents kept saying that I didn't have to go, because this is a long day of tests. Ye Ye will be moving to the rehab center soon, which is in another part of the hospital, where he'll stay while he gets better.

But I wanted to go. I wanted to keep Ye Ye company, and to be there with my Nai Nai and my dad. Plus, I figure it's probably best to start as soon as possible with his lessons, so there's that, too.

I found myself pausing when we got to the door of Ye Ye's room, and my stomach felt a little nervous. But I took a deep breath, and I reminded myself that it was going to be okay. I'm an Epic hero. And I was going to make everything better.

"Ye Ye!" I said, sailing into the room, wielding my notebook in front of me like a sword (because that's how you make a Dramatic entrance, as a hero). "How are you?" I asked, making sure to sound happy and upbeat so he would be too.

"Cilla," he said softly. He reached his hand out to me, and I took it, and he squeezed it. Which didn't answer the question, but I knew we'd get there. And speaking of which—

"I brought you a present!" I said, holding out my notebook. It was a brand-new blank one that Colleen had given me for my birthday. It was perfect, with a rainbow Steed (an Epic word for "horse") on the front.

"For soccer, Colleen uses Muscle Memory," I explained. "It means your body remembers things that your brain doesn't right away. Here—try writing something in English. Maybe the Muscle Memory will kick in!"

I was excited, and waited with a big smile for Ye Ye to answer, and take the pen and write, right then and there.

But Ye Ye just looked confused and asked my dad something in Chinese.

"Um, sweetheart," my dad said. "That's not really how it works." He saw how disappointed I looked and came over and put a hand on my shoulder. "I don't even know if he can hold the pen right now," he said, in a quieter voice.

"Oh," I said.

I hadn't considered that.

Suddenly, I realized that this was going to be harder than I thought.

I almost said so, too. But then I saw Ye Ye's face. And how sad, and kind of lost he looked, as my dad and I had a conversation that he clearly couldn't quite understand.

"Don't worry, Ye Ye," I said, going over to sit on the side of his bed. "We'll find another way. Here," I opened the notebook. "I'll draw a picture for you instead."

And he smiled and patted my hand, so I sat by him and drew.

Ye Ye wasn't actually in his room very long that day. He had lots of tests and scans and evaluations (all Synonyms, but also apparently all something different in hospitals), and I hadn't realized quite how long these would take.

My dad volunteered to keep Ye Ye company (which he explained, when I wanted to come, was really just sitting in waiting rooms).

So that left me and my Nai Nai. She smiled at me, and I took her hand.

I wanted to say something Wise or profound (a Synonym for "Wise"), that would let her know that everything was going to be okay, and I was going to help Ye Ye Triumph.

But my plan hadn't worked so well, and suddenly, I was less sure about how quickly I could make Ye Ye feel better.

Which I didn't really want to think about.

So I said the next best thing, which was, "Colleen told me that hospitals have surprisingly good soft serve. Also, we should eat the green Jell-O, but not the red or yellow."

"Wah," Nai Nai said, and even though she still looked tired, she smiled. "Soft serve before lunch? What an Adventure—let's go!"

And I grinned back, and took her hand, and we walked to the cafeteria.

She bought the soft serve, which was really nice of her, and once I'm allowed to Babysit and make money I promised I'd buy her some too, because soft serve is the greatest.

Ye Ye came back later in the afternoon, and he was—as my dad had said he'd be—very, very tired. But he motioned me over before we left, and I gave him a sort-of-hug and tried not to get caught in the tube in his arm or think about how the hospital-gown fabric was nothing like the warm, fuzzy sweater vests Ye Ye loves to wear that feel nice and soft when you hug him.

He didn't seem like my Ye Ye *at all*.

And I couldn't wait until he was back.

I thought about the hospital, and what had gone wrong, all afternoon. My parents kept saying things like "Everything okay, sweetie?" and "Do you want to talk, Cilla?" But I didn't. Because everything WASN'T okay, and there was nothing they could do—I'm the one who's going to make this right for Ye Ye. Plus I kept thinking about how tired my Nai Nai looked and how much it reminded me of my dad. I didn't want to add anything to their worries.

So I said no.

But, luckily, I got a *great* surprise, because the doorbell rang and it was my Grandma Jenkins, who had brought over a big pot of stew for Nai Nai at the hospital. My mom said, in this order:

1. Aw, thanks, Mom! You shouldn't have!
2. Mom, that's enough stew to feed a family for a week.
3. Do you want to stay for dinner? Why don't you have Dad drive over? And . . .
4. (Sigh) Yes, of course he can bring the dog.

This was all *excellent,* because it's hard to feel sad when there's a dog that's happy to see you and runs in and jumps on your lap and licks your face. And we all love Daisy, my grandparents' pug, even if my dad does say "Argh!" when she jumps on the couch and tries to lick his ears. But my mom says it's good for him, plus he's not allergic to Daisy (he's allergic to all cats and some dogs too), so there's no harm done.

My Grandma kept saying that I'm being "very brave," which was nice to hear, and hopefully true (because all Epic heroes are brave—it's a rule). Plus then there were other people there to help when Gwen got upset because she wanted to show my dad a dragon puppet she'd made in day care, but he had to answer the phone because it was Nai Nai.

This gave me some free time, so while all the adults were talking, I decided that I'd try to teach Daisy tricks, and she made *excellent* progress with jumping, especially when I held up pieces of stew for her to aim for. So I took this as proof that I'm a good teacher and that I'll get the hang of this eventually.

My grandparents left after dinner, Daisy whining behind them because she was sad to leave me (and all the stew I'd fed her).

And while I was helping my parents clean, I learned other things about pens. For example, that they can fly VERY fast through the air when Gwen throws them, because she found one on the ground and got mad because my mom and I were cleaning, and my dad was holding Essie, and she wanted attention. So then she threw it, and it hit the vase my mom hates but my dad loves, and the vase fell and broke. But my mom didn't seem to mind, and even said something like "About time" under her breath.

So it was funny, and my mom and I glued the pieces together (and found almost all of them—you can barely tell the vase was broken at all). We sat in the living room, and my dad bounced Essie, and my mom read a picture book to Gwen, and Gwen said the words she knew. I sat on the floor and drew more pictures in my journal and listened, because even though I'm in fifth grade, you're never too old to enjoy a good story.

And my pens worked just fine, even though Daisy, it seems, had gotten into my pencil case sometime earlier and chewed on them.

Which goes to show that the pen is actually pretty mighty (and impressively tough), after all.

6

A SUPER(HERO) STRATEGY

When I got to school today, I knew I needed help. If Muscle Memory (and a trusty Steed!) couldn't help Ye Ye, then I needed a plan, a strategy, a guaranteed way to teach English (and fast).

And I knew exactly who to turn to.

My mom had called the school, and all my friends' parents, to tell them what had happened. So Colleen had called me over the weekend to see how I was (and that's when she'd told me about the soft serve, too. See what I mean about her being a great friend? She always knows how to make things better).

Colleen has spent time in hospitals because her

grandma needed hip surgery, and Colleen and her family went to visit. So during morning worksheets, I told Colleen, Melissa, and Alien-Face all about the weekend, and that I'd already tried Muscle Memory and it hadn't worked (also, that the soft serve WAS good).

"Hmmm . . . ," Colleen said.

"Well," Melissa said, "I don't know about teaching English. But I spent some time in the hospital when my dad had knee surgery, and I know that if you can get Gwen to walk around with you and look sad and cute, all the nurses will give you Popsicles."

"AMAZING!" I said. And I felt lucky to have such Brave Companions.

"Also," Melissa went on, "When my Abuela has trouble with English words, we just act it out."

"That's what I do with my Nai Nai sometimes," I said. "But I've never done that with my Ye Ye, and I don't know . . ."

"Charades!" Alien-Face yelled, all of a sudden.

"You could play charades! Ye Ye would love that game, and maybe THAT'S how the Muscle Memory will kick in."

We all looked at him, impressed.

"Good plan, Alien-Face!" Colleen said.

"Yeah!" Melissa said.

"Brilliant," I said. Which is a Synonym for "Wise," but with an added layer of "excellent."

Just then, Ms. Paradise walked by.

"This doesn't sound like morning worksheets," she said.

"Sorry, Ms. Paradise," I said. "It's just that—"

"Now, Cilla," Ms. Paradise cut me off. "I know talking is fun, but morning exercises are important. So I'm going to need you to focus, okay? Remember: middle school Expectations!"

"But—" I started. She gave me a look. "Okay," I said softly.

"Okay," Colleen and Melissa and Alien-Face said.

"Great." Ms. Paradise clapped her hands, and swished away.

I put my head in my hands and sighed, and

Colleen patted my shoulder as we all turned to our morning worksheets.

I tried not to be too discouraged. Tricksters are hard to deal with. Plus all Quests have a "Challenges" phase, and I knew this was mine.

But I hoped it would be over soon.

I loved the charades idea, and I knew I'd try it once Ye Ye could move around a bit more. But I knew too that no matter how great and supportive my friends had been, there was probably only one person who could really help me. Because if a whole hospital of doctors can't give you an answer, there's only one place left to turn.

"Ms. Clutter," I said, as I burst into the library that day at recess. "I need you!"

"Cilla!" she said with a smile. "Of course. What's up?"

"I need help finding a book," I said.

"Great, what can I help you find? Mystery? Magic Adventure?"

"No," I said, though they were all great suggestions. "I need a book on how to teach English," I explained.

"Huh," Ms. Clutter said.

She leaned forward at the desk, and the beautiful gold scarf she was wearing over her hair that day rippled like waves as she did. (Only the best Similes for Ms. Clutter.)

She smiled in a nice, friendly way, and I *knew* she was about to say, "I have the PERFECT book for you and whoever you're teaching will learn English in NO time. Possibly today."

But instead, she said, "Everything all right, Cilla?"

"Yeah," I said quietly, after a minute.

"Do you want to talk about anything?" she asked.

I sort of did, but I sort of didn't, too, because how do you explain that you either have to teach your Ye Ye English or you'll lose him altogether?

"I just . . . I just need that book," I said.

"Well," she said, "I don't think I have anything like that here in the library right now, but I'll start looking today and will see what I find. We'll get you what you need."

"Okay," I said. I felt my face getting brighter.

"Okay," she said.

And I felt much better.

"So," Ms. Clutter said, "in the meantime, let's get you some reading material to hold you over. What do you think—time travel or epic bobsled adventure with dragons?"

"Epic Bobsled Adventure!" I said.

Which, short of a book to help me teach Ye Ye English RIGHT NOW, is probably the best thing I could ask for.

I got back to class just as everyone was coming in from recess. I started to tell Colleen what Ms. Clutter had said, but when the bell rang Ms. Paradise said, "Ring ring, middle school!" This is her new favorite thing, and it's supposed to remind us that in middle school, we'll only have a few minutes to switch classes before the bell rings. So we'll have to be focused and pack up our things quickly, and we can't talk with our friends.

We're supposed to practice it now and pretend we're in middle school when the bell rings, which makes no sense because shouldn't we try to get the talking out of our systems while we can? Especially if you can't even take a break from being Serious when you're in the hallway once you're in middle school (which sounds exhausting).

But even though I couldn't talk to Colleen just then, I knew I'd be able to tell her all about Ms. Clutter, and the book she'd given me, on the way home. And I knew no one would make fun of me for liking something with dragons, because we're still in elementary school (thank goodness). Plus

Mimi and Lisa carpool, which gives me a break from all my Foes on the bus.

So I felt better. And I was excited for journal writing, which always happens right after recess.

We were all deep into our writing, when, a few minutes later, the door of our classroom opened. Someone outside motioned to Ms. Paradise, who stuck her head out the door and began to whisper. Suddenly, Ms. Paradise said, "Oh!" And then she turned around and raced into the room.

"Cilla!" Ms. Paradise came rushing over to my desk. "I'm so sorry," she said, kneeling down so our heads were at the same level. "Your mom called this morning to tell us about your grandpa, but Mr. Usmani forgot to pass on the message. Ms. Clutter just happened to be in the office and spotted the note on his desk." She gave me a big, warm hug. "If you need to talk, I'm always here, okay?"

And even though Ms. Paradise isn't my favorite, I smiled at her, and a real smile this time. Because it was a really nice offer, even if I didn't want to talk just then. (And *especially* not to someone who says "There's a silver lining to every cloud" when anything bad happens. Which doesn't make a lot sense because clouds are made of water, not silver, so that sounds like pollution and not something you'd want.)

But I was glad she cared, all the same, Trickster or not.

And from the corner of my eye, I saw a flash of gold fluttering as the door closed: Ms. Clutter's scarf, waving behind her like a cape.

Ms. Moody, the guidance counselor, came to check on me later too, and said she was sorry for the mix-up. And when she asked how I was, I smiled and said okay, and meant it really and truly.

Because with Wise Guides who are also undercover superheroes like Ms. Clutter on my side, how can my Quest go wrong?

I was in a good mood the rest of the day. I even enjoyed band and didn't think about Mimi or Lisa once (especially because Mr. Kendall said that I was making the strongest sounds in the tuba section, so there).

And when I got home, I was ready to go visit Ye Ye.

"Ms. Clutter is helping me," I told Gwen as I put her toys in a backpack to bring to the hospital. "She's going to find books all about learning English again. And until she does, I have the best plan—books! I'll bring him some and read aloud to him!"

"Bwooks!" Gwen said. "I want bwooks! Read to me? Play?"

"Later," I promised. "But I'm glad you approve of my plan." I went to the bookshelf. "Let's start with . . . Selena Moon! It's the best series," I told Gwen as she started chewing on her Batman doll. "And book six, *Selena Moon and the Prophecy of the Waxing Crescent*, is SO GOOD, with SO MANY twists and turns. He won't be able to resist, he'll have to remember English if he wants to find out what happens."

"Yeah!" Gwen yelled.

"Yeah!" I said, because I thought this was a pretty excellent plan (if I do say so myself).

"Everything okay here?" my mom asked, coming downstairs with Essie dressed to go out.

"We're just making plans for Ye Ye," I said, showing her *Selena Moon*. "I'm going to read this to him."

"Um, sweetie," my dad said, peeking out from his office. "That might be a bit too much, for both of you."

"Why?" I asked, holding up my book (I had to use two hands, it's eight hundred pages).

"Well, it's kind of long," my dad said. "And Ye Ye might not understand."

"Oh, no, that's the point," I explained. "He'll listen, and then he'll start to understand."

"Yeah!" Gwen said. Then, "Cilla, fix Batman," because Batman's scrunchie tutu had fallen off.

"Of course," I said, and I tossed *Selena Moon* onto the coffee table.

"Caref—" my mom began. But I'd already dropped it down, and I'd maybe forgotten how heavy *Selena Moon* is and ... CRASH. The reglued vase went flying.

"Oops," I said, making an I'm-sorry face at my dad. "We can glue it again. Right, Mom?"

"Great," my dad said, rubbing the space between his eyes. (Incidentally, I think he needs new glasses, because he does this a lot.)

"Gweat!" Gwen said.

But my mom was too busy laughing to answer.

* * *

The lesson didn't go as well as I'd hoped. (But it's okay, I told Ye Ye. We have PLENTY of time—it's a loooooong book.)

I read Ye Ye the first few pages of *Selena Moon*, and he seemed to enjoy listening. But when I asked Reading Comprehension Questions (which are a big Theme in school, and sometimes kind of boring), he couldn't answer them. I don't even know if he understood them, which was too bad because I'd worked hard to make them REALLY exciting, like:

Is Selena's star pendant
  A. Purple
  B. Shiny
  C. All powerful and capable of summoning unicorns that will help her defeat evil once and for all in book 7 (Spoiler Alert)
  D. All of the above

Unfortunately Ye Ye couldn't answer (it's D by the way). But he asked me to keep reading because he thought my expressions were funny. So that's a start.

Gwen wanted to be a part of the story, too, so she sat on the side of the bed and played hand puppets with Ye Ye while I read, and my dad talked with the doctors, and my mom drove Nai Nai home to get some rest.

And even though we couldn't stay too long, because Ye Ye got tired, it was a nice visit.

Especially because, before we left, we put Melissa's Popsicle plan into action, and I helped Gwen get *exactly* the right expression (a blend between big, almost-crying eyes, and a wavering smile). So then there were A LOT of Popsicles to eat.

We said goodbye to Ye Ye and drove home. Just before dinner, my mom sat down on the couch, and Gwen went to get her book while I finished my homework and my dad played with Essie.

And everything felt like normal.

Until my dad's phone rang, and it was Nai Nai with an update for my dad.

He went into the other room, and my mom went to take Essie.

"Mommy, read?" Gwendolyn asked, toddling back, holding her book out.

"Of course, sweetie." My mom bent down to take it. But suddenly, Essie began to cry.

"Nath—" My mom turned to hand him Essie, then saw he was still on the phone. "One second, sweetie, okay?" she said to Gwendolyn, as she hoisted Essie up on her side. "Oh dear," she said, patting her bottom, "I think you're a bit of a mess . . . Can you keep an eye on Gwen, Cilla?" she asked as she left the room.

"Okay," I called after her, still keeping my eyes on my math homework.

Gwen watched my mom go, holding out the book to her as she walked away.

"Come on, Gwen," I said. "Sit by me and read."

Her bottom lip shook.

"Gwen, come on," I said, pulling myself up. "Come

play with your toys. Mom will read to you when she gets back."

"No!" she said. I sighed, and scooched next to her on the rug. "Fine," I said, reaching for the book, "Let's read."

She looked at me with big eyes that were filling with water, and not in a pretend way this time.

All of a sudden, I thought of Ms. Clutter. It had been so nice to talk to her today, and to have her know exactly what would make me feel better.

And it had been the nicest thing of all to know that she'd noticed I was upset. And had seen that something wasn't quite right.

"Oh!" I pretended to gasp, as if I'd just been surprised by the best thing ever.

"What?" she asked, startled.

"Well," I said, "I just realized you picked a book with a dragon in it. And you made that AMAZING dragon hand puppet in day care, right?"

"Oh!" she said.

"Should *she* read it to you?" I asked.

"Yeah!" Gwen ran over to get the puppet from

the dining room table, tears forgotten. And we read the book, and named her dragon puppet Flo, and decided that she'd be our best friend from then on, and would help us (and Batman) with any Adventures that came our way.

So all in all, I learned some excellent strategies today.

And it was mostly, and surprisingly, really nice.

Except for what I learned when I was trying to glue the vase back together AGAIN.

Which is that when something's been broken,

glued, then broken again, the pieces are even harder to fit back together.

But don't worry, I'll find a way.

I'm a future author extraordinaire, with a dragon puppet and a real, live undercover superhero on my side, after all.

FUHSTRATION

Sometimes I forget that English is my dad's second language, just like it's my Ye Ye's.

My dad came over from China with Ye Ye and Nai Nai when he was a little kid. He'd learned a few English words, because Ye Ye had lived in America before he was married and taught him some of what he knew (which is another reason he should have no problem getting his English back—he's known it for a LONG time).

But my dad had to learn most of the English he knows by himself, in school, once he was here. When he was only a little younger than I am now.

Which must have been hard.

Now my dad speaks English fluently. It's the

language he speaks most of the time, and he's told me that he even thinks and dreams in English.

But every once in a while he sometimes still makes small mistakes with the words he uses. Or says words a little differently.

And my favorite is "fuhstrated."

Fuhstrated is my dad's way of saying "frustrated." But when he says it, it's not the normal kind of frustration anymore. It's not the frustrated you feel because you have too much homework, or Daisy won't stop chewing on your socks. That's frustrated—when something's annoying but small, and you get over it pretty quickly. So you can do your homework, or try to train Daisy not to chew on socks (emphasis on "try"). And whether it works or not, you know that the problem will go away soon, and can mostly be solved.

But when my dad and I sigh in just the same way, and say, "Nothing's wrong, I'm just *fuhstrated!*" it means something else.

When you're fuhstrated, it means that every part of you is tired and doesn't know what to do. It means that nothing's right, and sometimes it means you're feeling sad or angry, but you're not sure at who, or what about. And it means that you don't, at all, even in the slightest, have the words to say all the things that you're feeling, and that there probably isn't anything that can make you, at least in this one particular moment, feel better.

This week started off as the opposite of fuhstrating, which means, it was actually going really well. We were getting ready for my Auntie Eva to visit again, and Ye Ye was doing so well at rehab. On Monday, I walked with him up and down the hallway, and even though he was slow and used his walker and couldn't do it for very long, he was still standing and walking and gripping with both hands. The doctors told us that he'll probably be able to go home really soon, because apparently you only spend a few weeks in hospital rehab, and then you do a lot of rehab work at home.

Which was all great, because even though Ye Ye hasn't made any breakthroughs in English, it will still be really nice to know that he's at home, where he belongs.

Ms. Clutter has found a few books for me, though none have been quite what I'm looking for. But she said they were the only ones she could find, and I have to admit, the English-Cantonese picture dictionary for English language learners was pretty impressive. Plus, as Ms. Clutter explained when she got it for me, "I know it's not quite right, but it's all we have right now, so I thought I'd give it to you. I bet you could learn some of the Chinese words so you can make sure he understands you while you teach."

"Great idea!" I said.

So when I went to visit Ye Ye after school on Tuesday we were using that, and Ye Ye was very nice and didn't laugh too hard at my pronunciation (Cantonese has NINE tones, which are hard to keep track of).

I'd come up with another great strategy too, because yes, maybe *Selena Moon* wasn't my best idea ever, because it's so long, and because so many of the words are made up anyway. And I realized I'd sort of gotten ahead of myself (which my mom says I do a lot, but I think a Synonym for that is just "good planning," which means it's mostly a strength, not something I have to change).

So instead, I'd decided to reteach him the ALPHABET.

Ye Ye loves to sing and seemed to like this new approach to teaching. He mostly just hummed the tune, but he was really into it and sat up and waved his hands around with me, so it was a good strategy in general. The only real challenge will be making sure he learns the RIGHT version, because Gwen is ALSO very excited about the alphabet, but also has some learning to do. So when we started singing, Gwen heard us from the hallway, where she'd been playing with my Nai Nai, and burst into the room, singing out her own VERY loud ABCs (with accompanying Interpretive Dance), which went something like:

ACDCBFO

PNMXQR . . . WHOAH!!

"Don't listen, Ye Ye!" I shouted. And then, "Also, not quite, Gwen. But GREAT rhymes." I smiled at her. "You'll get there eventually, don't worry."

Gwen beamed up at me, and I hoped my dad had noticed, because I'm a Very Supportive Sister and should really be Babysitting all the time at this point.

We spent the rest of our visit singing, and Ye Ye's roommate, Ronnie, is so nice because he didn't mind at all, and in fact, asked one of nurses to bring us Popsicles (which is the mark of a very good kind of person).

"Just wait till next time, Ye Ye," I said with a big smile as we got ready to go, and my dad translated for me. "And if this doesn't work, I'll find another strategy—I know we'll get there!"

Ye Ye grinned and said something in Chinese.

"He can't wait," my dad said.

So as you can see, things were going really well. And I was very hopeful.

Until school on Wednesday, which is when the fuhstration began.

It all started at recess. The morning had been good, and lunch had been French toast sticks (which is always a sign of a good day).

We'd all giggled and joked together because Ms. Paradise has a new Theme, which is Teamwork. So she keeps saying things like, "We're a team, and a good team works together!" Or "Ask yourself—is this a team problem or a Ms. Moody problem?" When she talks about what to do if we're upset or have fights or get mad at each other.

And it's funny because (1) teams are great, but I'm never going to like Mimi Donnelly, and *definitely* don't think she's on my team, and (2) Ms. Moody is nice (and surprisingly cheerful, despite her name), but does she really want us to bug her every time Jeff steals Alien-Face's hat and won't give it back and they sort-of-fight but sort-of-play at recess? I don't think so.

Anyway, as we left lunch, we were laughing about Ms. Paradise's new sayings, which include "Team is tantamount" and "Teamwork makes the dream work." (Sigh.)

Colleen had to stay behind for a few minutes for a yearbook meeting. So Melissa and I ran excitedly out to the field to check on our fairy houses from the week before (they always fall apart, and we like to pretend it's from the fairies using them to have giant dance parties, not the wind, rain, and snow, which is more likely).

We were playing and laughing and having such a good time that we barely noticed when the yearbook committee came walking out of the building.

"Hey, guys!" Colleen called, waving and heading in our direction.

"Oh, Colleen!" I said, leaping to my feet and brushing grass off my jeans.

Colleen came running toward us, though when she walked by the climbing structure and the kids playing there, she veered away, taking a long way around.

I wondered why, and was going to ask her.

But then I saw that there were other members of the yearbook committee also coming toward us.

And walking with Sasha was Mimi Donnelly.

"What are you guys doing?" Colleen asked.

"Um," I said. Mimi stopped at the edge of the playground, right where she could hear us.

"Well," Melissa said, "We—"

"Nothing much," I said quickly, cutting her off. "Just some Silly kids' stuff."

"Oh," Melissa said.

"Well, Sasha wanted to play kickball," Colleen said. "Do you want to play, Melissa? You could coach us, Cilla, or come and watch and cheer."

"Um," I said.

"Sure," Melissa said quietly. "I'll play. Meet you at the field." And she walked away from us without saying another word, toward the kickball field.

"Are you okay?" Colleen looked at me, puzzled, and at Melissa's back.

"Yeah," I said, even though that was NOT how I was feeling. "You go play, Colleen," I said. "I don't mind."

Colleen frowned like she was trying to figure something out. But she couldn't.

"Okay," she said finally. "I'll see you in a bit."

She went racing over to join the others, and I waved because I didn't want her to think I was upset or anything.

But I felt a hard, bad feeling in my stomach. Because I knew I'd hurt Melissa's feelings.

I thought I'd go see if Alien-Face wanted to play, but he was on the monkey bars with Tim #1, and he looked so happy, I didn't want to bother him.

I thought about sitting on the swings on my own. But that didn't feel fun, plus all I could think about was who was watching me, and what Mimi would say when she heard I'd been sitting by myself.

"Can I go to the library early?" I asked Mr. McKinstry, the recess monitor.

"Sure," he said. "You feeling oka—Hey, no running up the slide, Josh, you know that...." He dashed away toward the third graders. It seemed like permission enough, so I made my way toward the school building.

I was just at the door when I heard my name.

"Cilla!"

I turned.

It was *Mimi Donnelly*.

"Um...," I stammered, trying to hide my surprise. "Hi," I said.

"Hi." She jogged to catch up with me and then stopped. "I, uh, liked your story in writing yesterday," she said quietly, like she was trying to find the right thing to say. "I thought the plot twist with the goblin was cool. Everyone else's was kind of boring."

"Thanks," I said. I wondered what she wanted.

"I...." She paused. "I just wanted to know if you'd like to hang out," she said, in one quick burst. "Lisa and Amanda aren't here, and I was going to hang out with Sasha, but now she's playing kickball with Melissa and Colleen. And, I dunno, we could go to the swings. Selena Moon and the Jenny Ojukwo series are my favorite books too. Have you read the newest Jenny book?"

I wasn't sure what to say. I LOVE talking about Selena Moon and Jenny Ojukwo, and even though I'd tried to pretend I didn't, I actually also liked Mimi's stories in writing (hers had been about a talking stone lion, and it was *excellent*, and I really wanted to know what happens).

But then I remembered who I was talking to.

She probably just wanted to find funny things to tell Lisa and Amanda about me later. Plus she was going to make fun of my story-making and the books I like and think they were for little kids.

"Sorry," I said quietly. "I'm not going to stay at recess today. I'm just going to the library."

"Oh, okay." Mimi looked down.

"See you later," I mumbled, also looking down. Then I turned and walked into the building.

It was all very strange, because I knew I was going to one of my favorite places, and Mimi isn't my friend anyway, she's a FOE. Which means I'm supposed to defeat her and DEFINITELY not supposed to feel bad for her. Plus it's not like I was mean to her or anything—I just wanted to sit and read.

But even knowing all these things, walking away and leaving Mimi all by herself on the cement sidewalk in front of the playground didn't feel great.

Which was fuhstrating.

It was just Ms. Clutter and our assistant librarian, Ms. Goia, in the library. (For the record, Ms. Clutter was wearing another AMAZING scarf—it was silver, and it swept around her face and down her back, and her glasses were silver to match. I bet they can also shoot lasers if she needs to, to defend the school from the Forces of Darkness, but that's just a guess.)

"Cilla!" Ms. Clutter said as she saw me. "You're here early."

"Yeah," I said, a little shyly. "Mr. McKinstry said I could come."

"Didn't feel like recess?" she asked.

I shook my head, and I hoped she wouldn't ask me more, because I REALLY didn't want to talk about it.

"I understand," she said. "Just one of those days, huh?"

I nodded and smiled. I can always count on Ms. Clutter to understand me.

I found a book and went to sit in a squishy blue armchair in the corner of the library. Usually when I read, I can't hear other things. So if someone's having a conversation, it won't distract me—in fact, I might not even notice it's happening.

But maybe it was the fuhstration, or maybe it was the name of some of my favorite books of all time. Because I'd only just started getting into my story, when I heard—

"Like the Selena Moon series?" Ms. Goia asked.

"Exactly," Ms. Clutter said. "We'll have a 'If you liked Selena Moon, you'll like' List. That gives the kids another source of books, other than the color-code system."

"I love it," Ms. Goia said. "Let's see. Selena Moon is fantasy, so maybe the Dark Machinery series?"

"Oh, not that!" I said, before I realized that I was listening in to their conversation (which my mom says is rude, even though she does it all the time), and interrupting (which is *very* rude, and much less fun than listening in on conversations). "Oh, sorry." I smiled sheepishly, worried they'd be angry.

"No, no, go on," Ms. Clutter said. "You don't think that's a good book for the list?"

"No," I said. "No offense, Ms. Goia—I LOVE the Dark Machinery series. But Selena Moon is all about magic and magic spells, and Dark Machinery is more about inventions, and there's only magic at the end. So a reader might be disappointed and stop reading, if they were expecting a story just like Selena Moon. But there are so many other books that could grab them in from the very beginning, like the Jenny Ojukwo series, or Annalee Appletree. And they have magic AND brave heroines, just like Selena Moon, and there are five books in the Jenny Ojukwo series. So I think it's better for your list, because it will encourage readers, and they'll try new things."

"Wow, thank you, Cilla." Ms. Clutter smiled, and I was relieved to see that Ms. Goia was also smiling, so she wasn't mad that I hadn't liked her idea. "That's really helpful. Hey," Ms. Clutter said, "do you want to help us with these lists? We could really use expertise like yours."

"Really?!" I asked, leaping up, my fuhstration forgotten.

Because this was AMAZING.

"Absolutely!" Ms. Clutter said. "Pull over a chair." I sat down at the table with Ms. Clutter and Ms. Goia (which felt VERY grown-up).

"Now," Ms. Clutter went on. "They can't all be long books—we need lists that students who might have trouble with reading will also be able to enjoy."

"I understand." I nodded. "I had a really hard time learning to read."

"Really?" Ms. Clutter asked, and she looked surprised.

"Yeah," I said with a smile. "I definitely have some suggestions. The trick is to have a book that's interesting and Dramatic, but short enough that you don't get discouraged and want to throw it . . ."

I spent the rest of recess with Ms. Clutter and Ms. Goia, talking about books.

Which makes the world feel like a much nicer place. No matter how fuhstrated you maybe were before.

After recess I went back to class. For the rest of the day I tried to be extra nice to Melissa.

And Melissa smiled back, so it seemed maybe all right.

I was feeling better. I started to think about all the things I could do to make everything okay, and how maybe I'd bring Melissa candy tomorrow. And Auntie Eva was going to be there when I got in, and I couldn't wait to tell her about Ms. Clutter, and about how I was helping a librarian make a reading list, and—"Cilla," my dad came racing out the front door, the phone tucked under his ear. "I'm sorry, sweetie, I meant to meet you at the bus."

"Hi, Dad!" I said. "Where's Auntie Eva? Also I have so much to tell you and I need your advice, and—"

"Of course," he said. "But first, I need to get to the hospital. Ye Ye's okay, but he's had a fall."

I felt like you do when a gym ball hits you in the stomach.

"What?" I asked.

"He'll be absolutely fine," my dad said. "Auntie Eva's there with him now. It's not anything serious— it's just a setback."

"But how did that happen?" I asked. He's been doing so well, and he's using his walker, and—"

"These things happen sometimes, Cilla," my dad said. "Ye Ye got a bit impatient, and you know how stubborn he can be. But the doctors were right there to help him. We just have to figure out what this means for him in the long run, that's all."

"Okay," I said quietly.

"Now, I need to go pick up Auntie Eva. But your Grandma Jenkins is here to watch you all."

"Can't I come with you?" I asked.

"Well, it's mostly going to be driving. I might not even see Ye Ye—he's resting."

"I'd just like to be there," I said. "If that's okay."

My dad put his hand on my shoulder.

"Of course."

I was quiet in the car. My dad asked me about my day, but I didn't really want to talk about it, no matter how much he said, "No, really, sweetie, I'd love to know. Did anything exciting happen? How was school? What advice do you need?"

But I just kept saying, "It was okay. Just a normal day."

Because all the good feelings from Ms. Clutter

had gone away. And all the bad feelings about Melissa were still bad, but felt silly to talk about, knowing Ye Ye had fallen.

My dad stopped asking questions after a while. But just as we turned into the hospital, he looked at me and smiled.

"You know," he said, "we should do something special one of these days, just the two of us. What do you think? Father-daughter day? Maybe we can go to the aquarium."

"Yeah!" I said, clapping my hands. "That would be amazing."

"Perfect," my dad said.

When we turned down Ye Ye's hallway, Auntie Eva was there.

"Auntie Eva!" I ran to her, and she lifted me off the ground in a big hug.

"Cilla!" she said. "I'm so glad you came. Are you doing okay?"

"Yeah," I said. "Are you?"

"Yes," she said. "Everything's fine; Dad's just going to need to stay a bit longer, that's all."

"Why don't you sit in one of the hall chairs, Cilla," my dad said. "Eva and I will get things settled, and then we can see if Ye Ye's up to saying hello."

"Oh, there's the nurse," Auntie Eva said.

So she and my dad went to go talk to her, leaving me in the hallway outside of Ye Ye's room.

I knew I should go sit down. But the door was open. So I peeked in.

I heard voices behind the white curtain.

And even though I knew I shouldn't, I walked a few steps in, so I could see past it.

Ye Ye was lying in bed, looking tired and pale, and Nai Nai was sitting next to him, and they were *arguing.*

Ye Ye had a hand over his eyes, and was pinching at them.

I realized he was CRYING.

"Cilla," my dad, whispered behind me, pulling me back. "Ye Ye's a bit frustrated, okay? Let's just give him some space."

"Okay," I said softly.

*　*　*

I sat in the hallway by myself while my dad and Auntie Eva talked with the doctors and nurses. And I wondered just how many Struggles heroes have to go through. In Ms. Stauffer's class, we learned about a hero who had to go through twelve Trials before his Epic was over, which is A LOT. So compared to him, I should feel lucky.

But this is the hardest Struggle I've ever had to deal with.

And I wished I was Wise, all on my own, and could make it all better, right then and there.

When I was allowed to go back in later, Ye Ye seemed okay. He gave me a hug, and said, "Ngoh oi neih."

He said something in Chinese to my dad, in the Confused Voice he has a lot now.

"He wants to know if you understood, Cilla," my dad said, patting his shoulder in a calming way.

"Of course," I said. And I bent down for one more sideways hug and put my arm across him.

"Ngoh oi neih, Ye Ye," I said.

My mom stopped by to bring Nai Nai some dinner, and Gwen came in with her and gave Ye Ye a kiss on the cheek.

While the adults said goodbye and planned who was going to sit with Ye Ye tomorrow, I sat with Gwen on the plastic chairs in Ye Ye's room and taught her how to say "ngoh oi neih" too. (Though quietly, because Ye Ye was asleep.)

"Woh eye knee!" she yell-whispered. Which was very close on both the Chinese and sound volume counts.

"Great job, Gwen," I whispered back. "I love you too."

Then she giggled (but quietly) and whispered, "Cilla, do Batman!"

So then I was Batman (but on a silent, stealth

mission). Batman swooshed, and dipped, and Gwen gave me whispered suggestions for what he should do, and the crimes he should stop, and the people he should save.

I drove home with my dad and Auntie Eva and Gwen, while my mom went to the grocery store to get food for dinner. Gwen fell asleep, which she always does in the car. And even though it was still (sort of) daytime, that didn't seem like the worst idea.

I closed my eyes and thought about all the things that had happened that day. I wasn't asleep, but I must have looked it, because Auntie Eva and my dad began to talk. The kind of talk that I don't think they'd say if they knew I was listening.

"Wow," Auntie Eva said softly. "I've never seen Dad cry before."

"Yeah," my dad said with a sigh.

"It's probably good that he's acknowledging it," Auntie Eva said. "It's just hard to see him so upset. Thank you, by the way, big brother." I opened my eyes a tiny crack, and saw her put an arm on his shoulder. "You've been a hero during all of this."

"Aw, happy to be here, sis. Don't worry, we'll get him back to a good place."

"Yeah. Do you think it will ever be the same,

though? Do you think we should look into options, for care?"

"I don't know." My dad sighed. "Ellen and I have talked about it. But I just don't think they'll agree to move."

"Maybe a nurse."

"Maybe," he said. "I didn't think we'd have to think about this just yet, you know? They're so young. But maybe things will turn around."

The conversation made me feel strange.

Sometimes I even forget that Ye Ye's their dad, the one who carried them around, and bounced them when they cried, and helped them with their math homework.

It's a funny thing to remember.

And it was scary to hear them talk this way.

So I decided to stop listening. Instead, I closed my eyes again, and tried to think of other, happier things. Of the Epic journey that *would* make everything better. Of having Auntie Eva there. Of all the helpful people around me: Ms. Clutter, the doctors and nurses, and Gwen, and Nai Nai, and my dad, and my mom, and even Batman. Who had stayed back at the hospital.

Because even in the face of Fuhstrations and Trials and all the Struggles of being a hero, it turns out that Batman and Gwen are also very Wise.

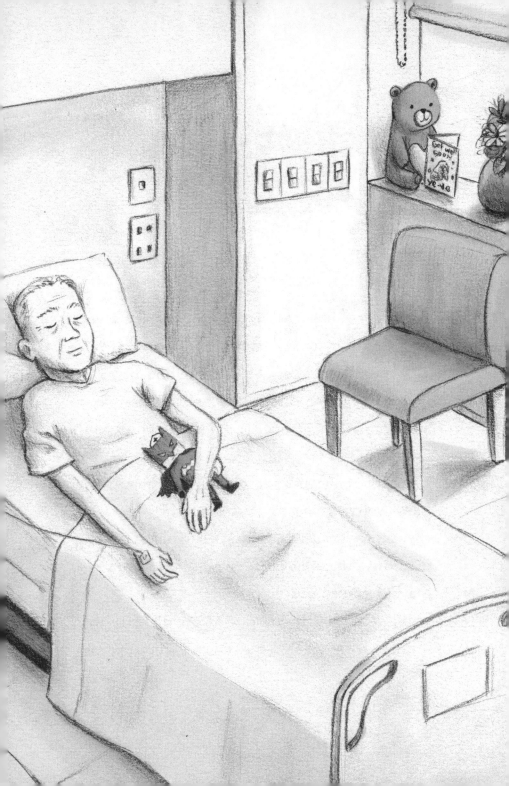

TAKE CARE

"Take care" is something my mom calls "a very Chinese" thing to say. It's what Nai Nai and Ye Ye and their friends are ALWAYS telling us to do. Sometimes "take care, take care" means "you're swinging too high!" or "the sidewalk is icy, don't fall!" Or if you're trying to walk on top of the monkey bars, it means "get down right now, Young Lady—you're going to hurt yourself." And when they say it when you're taking a pan out of the oven it means "that's hot, use a potholder," and also maybe "let me do it."

So even though there are lots of different ways it can be meant, it all comes down to the same idea.

It means "be careful." And even more than that, it means "I'll take care of you."

It seems simple.

But I'm learning that taking care is actually a really hard thing to do.

Which is strange to discover.

Ye Ye's had SO many visitors recently. Lots of people come, and friends from Chinatown and the community center visit, and sit with him, and bring him soft foods (there's TONS of tapioca pudding, which is excellent because I love it too, and Ye Ye is a great sharer). All around his walls are cards from friends, and his windowsill is always filled with flowers. And Auntie Stella and Uncle Gerard made friends with Ronnie and even bring him flowers, too. So their entire room is bright and beautiful.

Seeing all these things makes me happy. I'm glad Ye Ye has his friends, and that they can make him smile, and it's great to see them and say hello.

But I also know that they can all speak to him in Chinese, and I can't.

So really, they're better at taking care of him than I am.

Ms. Paradise and Ms. Moody, and Mom and Dad, and my Nai Nai, Grandma, and Grandpa all keep saying things like "Do you want to talk about anything? Is there anything I can do to help?"

But the answer is "no," because unless they have a magical orb that teaches you English when you touch it I don't think there's anything anyone can do.

Ye Ye hasn't been upset since I saw him that day. He's making progress, the doctors say. And lots of days, after school, I go to visit him. Some days I try to teach him vocabulary, and do charades, which he thinks are funny. But they haven't worked quite yet. Plus it can be hard because we get interrupted a lot, by things like doctors and nurses and physical therapy and speech therapy.

But we've had fun times too. One day, I brought my tuba to the hospital to show him my progress. Gwen danced around and sang the Batman song, waving him in the air while I played. (I was playing the "Macarena," not the Batman song, but she made it work.) And Ye Ye waved his arms around and danced, which made Essie laugh and giggle and drool on his sweater.

This weekend, I wasn't planning on going to the hospital. I was sleeping over at my Grandma and Grandpa Jenkins's house, and it was just me, which was nice, because even though I enjoy being an older sister (and am excellent at it), sometimes it's nice to have your grandparents to yourself, and to be able to do what you want to do.

The timing was great, too, because I could ask Grandma Jenkins for teaching advice.

"Why?" she asked.

"No reason." I shrugged. "I just want to know."

Grandma Jenkins has been teaching college students for a long time. College is even older than middle school, so also scary. But happily, when my Epic's done I'll be so grown-up that I'll be ready for that too, so I won't have to worry. (I plan ahead like that.)

Grandma Jenkins had A LOT of tips that I'm filing away for later. Some Ye Ye already has down, like students needing to learn to take responsibility for themselves (he's great at this). But she also said that students should have homework due on a regular basis, and get lots of feedback through things like grading, which is very helpful.

"So," Grandma Jenkins said a little while later, as we mixed cookie batter, "how are you doing, Cilla? I know things have been tough with Ye Ye in the hospital."

"Yeah," I said with a sigh. "I'm okay."

She gave me a sideways look.

"You know, Cilla, you never have to talk about it if you don't want to. But it's all right not to be okay. It's also all right to tell people, and to ask for help, if you want it."

"Hm," I said. I was quiet for a few minutes. She was quiet too, and even though she kept looking over at me like she was wondering about something, she didn't say anything else, which I appreciated. It was a lot to think about.

"I can't wait for the cookies," I said, after a few minutes. "If we have leftovers, can I take some home for Nai Nai?"

"Of course," Grandma Jenkins said. "How is Rachel?" (This, by the way, is my Nai Nai, and it's pretty Epic itself that she and Grandma Jenkins are on a First-Name Basis, which is a BIG DEAL for adults. See my first book for this story.)

"She's okay—" I began. But then I stopped. Nai Nai says she's okay. She's always smiling when visitors are around. But she also looks tired a lot of the time. Like you can see all the worry she's feeling.

"Well," I said. "She says she's okay. But she's really tired, I think. Dad and Ye Ye keep trying to get her to spend some days at home, but she won't. She goes in to sit with Ye Ye every day; she's been at the hospital this whole time. If dad's there, she'll go out for a bit, but otherwise—Grandma?"

Grandma Jenkins had stopped mixing the batter.

"Change of plans, Cilla," she said. "Get your grandfather—we're going out."

So all of a sudden we were at the *hospital*: me, Grandpa Jenkins, and Grandma Jenkins.

"Hello, Rachel," Grandma Jenkins said, giving Nai Nai a big hug. "Hello, Lester," she said, giving Ye Ye a hug in the chair where he was sitting.

"What a surprise!" Nai Nai said. "I'm so glad you're here."

"Well," Grandma Jenkins said, "I'm not staying long, and neither are you. We're going out—you, me, and Cilla. Edgar will sit with Lester."

"Oh," Nai Nai said. "Well . . ."

Ye Ye took her hand and said something in Chinese. I knew that even though he didn't completely understand what Grandma Jenkins had said, he agreed with her.

Nai Nai hesitated.

"We'll have a grand ole time," Grandpa Jenkins said, trying to help. "Why, we can order a pizza and watch the game!"

"Um, Ye Ye can't have pizza," I said. "Also he doesn't watch sports."

"Nonsense," Grandpa Jenkins said. "If we can't get pizza, chocolate cake! Can he eat that?"

"Uh," Nai Nai said, but she was smiling now. "Not that either," she said. She gave Ye Ye an affectionate pat. "He complains about it every day."

"So does Grandpa Jenkins if he doesn't get cake—" I said.

"Just like Edgar—" Grandma Jenkins said at the same time.

We giggled, because it was true.

"Well, that settles it," Grandma Jenkins clapped her hands. "They'll have a lot to talk about. Let's go!"

I gave Ye Ye a hug, and Nai Nai gave him a kiss on the cheek, and he said something in Chinese that I knew meant "have a wonderful time." And we pretended not to hear as Grandpa Jenkins whispered to Ronnie as we left, "What about chocolate pudding? He can have that, right?"

So that was how Grandma Jenkins, Nai Nai, and I went out for the afternoon.

We had cake at a fancy café, and Grandma Jenkins and Nai Nai talked about flowers and their gardens and told me stories about all the trouble they got into as kids (which was AMAZING to learn). Then we went to get our nails painted, which felt super fancy, and I've never done that before at a store, and Grandma Jenkins let me get neon green, which made me REALLY happy.

We got back to the hospital a few hours later. Just before we walked into the room, Grandma Jenkins took Nai Nai's hand.

"You know, Rachel," she said, "you have to take care of yourself."

"I know," Nai Nai said, squeezing Grandma Jenkins's hand. "It's just hard."

"Of course," Grandma Jenkins said. "Well, we'll just have to visit more, to give you a break."

"That would be wonderful," Nai Nai said with a smile.

So hand in hand, they walked back in together.

* * *

"Wow, Grandma," I said, as we got back in the car, to go home. "You're very Wise."

"Well, you don't get to my age without being a little Wise, kid," she said with a smile.

I smiled back, because I was VERY impressed. And it's a reassuring thought, because I'll at least have Wisdom *someday*.

That night, Grandma Jenkins cooked my favorite dinner. Grandpa Jenkins surprised us with chocolate cake and mint ice cream, my favorite dessert, from the bakery down the road.

After dinner, we sat together, quietly, all reading. I snuggled up with Grandma Jenkins on the couch, and Grandpa Jenkins sat in his special armchair. It was so nice to just spend time together, and to say "Golly!" when the mystery took a twist (Grandpa Jenkins) or "My heavens!" when an interesting fact came up in her history book (Grandma Jenkins), or to laugh and then read a paragraph aloud so everyone could enjoy it when the book got really funny (me). And Daisy spent the whole time curled up on my lap, sleeping and sometimes waking up to lick my nose, then going back to sleep.

And just then, as hard as things can sometimes be, it was nice to know we were all taking care, in the best ways we knew how.

MATURITY IS HARD,
BUT COOKIES ARE GREAT

Getting older is complicated.

There are so many things to look out for, like people who say there are boys' things and girls' things (see: the tuba). Growing up also means that certain things feel harder. So, for example, it feels more complicated sometimes to have conversations now that we're older.

When I was in first grade, Colleen and I had our first big fight. Later, we realized that we were both wrong, and we both said sorry, and we both said it's okay, and then we hugged, and that was that.

But now that we're older, I'm realizing that "I'm

sorry" can be harder. In fact, it can be a pretty big Trial all its own.

Because Melissa didn't do anything wrong. I did.

On Monday, I told Melissa I was sorry.

She smiled and said, "It's okay." But she hadn't suggested we go and play in the field with our fairy houses since.

And I didn't really know how to make it better.

If life were normal, the person I'd ask would be Ye Ye. It's not that the rest of my family doesn't give good advice (my Grandma Jenkins, as I've mentioned, is VERY Wise). But when it comes to school and my friends, Ye Ye's the one who's always really understood me. Plus, after my visit at their house, Grandma and Grandpa Jenkins went away for the week. So even if I'd wanted to ask them for advice, right now, I couldn't.

On top of all that, everyone else is so busy. My dad is helping Nai Nai get the apartment ready for Ye Ye to come home, and when he's not, he's working and running around, saying things like, "Argh, why does Excel never work?" My mom has a lot of work projects too, and between Gwen and Essie, and my homework, and helping my dad with Ye Ye, I know they're both busy. And I don't want to worry them.

So I felt sort of on my own with this one.

But weirdly, I *wasn't* on my own with another problem. An actually much worse problem, that also happened at the very beginning of the week.

We had just gotten out to recess, and Colleen ran ahead of us to tell Sasha that she wouldn't be playing kickball today because Melissa had a new origami pattern to teach us.

Melissa and I found a place by the side of the school and waved to Colleen as she came jogging back to join us, through the shortcut between the field and the climbing structure, and the boys who always played there.

Just then, I remembered that, for some reason, she'd been avoiding the climbing structure.

And as she ran by, one of the boys there said something. His friends laughed.

Colleen's expression changed, just for a moment, like she was upset. But then she froze. Her face was, all of a sudden, blank.

Melissa and I looked at each other and frowned.

"Colleen," I said, as she reached us. "Is everything okay? What did he just say?"

"It's nothing." Colleen shrugged. "Let's go play."

"It didn't look like nothing," Melissa said. Which is a BIG statement for Melissa, because she's like me, and we don't like to disagree or fight with people.

"They just . . . they made fun of my hair," Colleen said, touching one of her braids. "It doesn't matter. This boy just said it was dirty, and, well . . . gross."

"Colleen, that's awful!" I said. Then, "Has this been happening a lot?"

She shrugged like it didn't bother her, but I know Colleen, and I knew she was pretending.

"A few times," she said. "It's no big deal."

"But . . . I think it's a big deal," Melissa said.

"Yeah," I said. "I think so too."

"Why didn't you tell us?" Melissa asked.

Colleen crossed her arms. "I dunno," she said. "He's younger than us, so I figured I shouldn't let it bother me. And I didn't want people to think I was immature, or Silly, because I couldn't take care of it on my own. We're fifth graders, after all."

I looked at my best friend. The person who's there for me and who I'm supposed to be there for. But this whole time I'd had no idea that this was happening.

She'd been keeping all that inside her, and all because she'd thought she needed to deal with everything on her own.

Suddenly, it occurred to me that even though I think of Colleen as the strongest, bravest warrior, and someone who can defeat any dragon, she still has her own Quests, and Struggles, and Trials.

And I realized that, maybe, she didn't have to go through those alone.

"You know, Colleen," I said, "my Ye Ye says that when things like this happen, it's their problem, not yours. But," I went on, "I think it's really actually and truly . . ."

At the same time we ALL said it, me, Melissa, and Colleen: "A Ms. Moody problem."

"Also, maybe you should also talk to your mom," Melissa said. "That's what I do."

"Yeah?" Colleen said.

"Yeah," I said.

And even though I couldn't talk to Ye Ye about this, and couldn't ask him about it, I knew he'd have said yes too.

And I was really proud of Colleen when, that night, she told her mom and dad what had happened.

There were a lot of meetings after that. Colleen and her mom and dad met with Ms. Moody, and then Colleen and her parents and the boy and his parents met with Ms. Moody. And according to Colleen, his parents made him apologize A LOT.

"Are you okay?" I asked Colleen, the day after one of the meetings at recess.

"Yeah," she sighed. "It's just a lot."

"It is a lot," I said. "But I'm here if you need me."

It was funny to actually be the one saying it, for once.

And to realize that I really and truly meant it.

There was nothing I could do for Colleen but to be there for her.

So I hoped she'd tell me if there was anything she wanted to talk about.

* * *

The next week was the week I'd been dreading all year long. It was the day of the middle school visit.

I knew there would be four seventh graders coming. I imagined a four-headed dragon stalking into our classroom, and I wondered if it would be an evil one, or the friendly kind that you share your snacks with and then it likes you, or, at least, decides not to eat you right away. In fact, I wondered if I could bring in cookies to appease them (it happens a lot in stories). But my mom said there was no time to bake, and the only other cookies we had at home were the gross ones my dad gets from the health store, and that wasn't going to help get middle schoolers—or anyone—to like me.

So in the end, it was just me, no cookies, in class, sitting next to Colleen and Melissa and Alien-Face McGee.

We sat at our desks after math, and waited. The classroom felt hot and stuffy, and everyone was quiet, which is unusual.

The door opened.

I took a deep breath, and reminded myself to be Serious and not make up stories, or say anything that they'd think was Silly or Immature. Ms. Paradise said, "Come on in!" And I prepared for what was about to come—four students, or an evil four-headed lizard monster, or a friendly four-headed dragon, or—

"Hey, is that your sister?"

One of the middle schoolers pointed as they filed in, and another smiled and began to wave.

I turned to where she was waving. There, blushing, and looking embarrassed and uncomfortable, but also looking at the seventh graders with big, impressed eyes was *Mimi Donnelly.*

"Hi, Meems!" the waving middle schooler said.

"Hi, Hattie," Mimi said shyly.

Colleen and I looked at each other, *shocked.*

Because they had the same smile, and the same expression in their eyes.

But it was more than that, too.

Mimi was looking at the middle schooler like she really wanted to impress her.

Because this smiling, friendly-looking middle school girl was Mimi Donnelly's older sister.

And somehow it hadn't occurred to me that if she had an older sister, it meant Mimi Donnelly was a *little sister*. Just like Gwen.

Which, for some reason, I found very surprising.

The middle school visit was actually kind of fun. A boy in a rainbow-striped shirt named Abdullah told us that all the teachers are friendly, and everyone will help you get around the hallways if you can't figure something out. A boy with hair in his eyes named Travis told us about how, in sixth grade, the teachers design big projects—in science we'll do a star journal, where we have to go out every night for a month and look at the constellations, and in history we'll go on a field trip to see how clothes used to be made. And at the very end, Hattie told us all about the clubs we could join, like Mathalon, and how we could play sports, but also join art club, language club, and even a *writing* club.

The middle schoolers seemed nice. And afterward, they even stayed for a few minutes to talk with us.

I thought about going to ask Hattie (Donnelly!) about the writing club. But I felt shy. And I was afraid of saying the wrong, un-Serious thing. So I just hovered with a group of fifth graders and listened while some of them asked questions. Mimi went to stand next to her sister, and Hattie talked with Tim #2 and Gabrielle, and anytime Hattie laughed, Mimi laughed too. When another middle schooler asked Mimi if she was nervous, I heard her say in a slightly too-loud voice, "Oh, no, I'm not nervous AT ALL," as she looked at her sister with big, kind of hopeful eyes. And every once in a while she looked toward Lisa and her other friends, like she was making sure they liked what she'd said.

And for the first time in all of fifth grade, I understood Mimi Donnelly.

* * *

The middle schoolers left and I waved goodbye with the rest of Ms. Paradise's fifth-grade class. I felt better, now that I'd met them. But I was still glad that we weren't in middle school just yet. Because being Serious is a lot of pressure. And I'm still not sure how I'm going to do it ALL THE TIME next year. (Plus I still sort of wished I'd brought cookies, because even though they seemed nice, four-headed dragons are tricky.)

We were still talking about the middle school visit when we went out to recess that day.

"Wow!" Colleen said, leaning against the school wall. "Mimi Donnelly was trying *so hard* to impress her sister."

"I know," Melissa said. "I think she's actually really nervous about middle school."

"Right?" I said.

"Like me!" Melissa and I said at the same time.

"Yeah," Colleen said, just after us. "Like me!"

"WHAT?!" Melissa and I turned to look at Colleen, shocked. "But you keep saying you're excited about it," I said.

"Yeah," Melissa said. "And you're so good at being grown-up!"

"Well," Colleen said with an almost embarrassed kind of smile, "I'm excited about some parts of middle school. But really, I was just saying all those things because . . . well, because I'm actually kind of terrified."

"Us too!" Melissa and I both said.

We were all quiet for a moment.

And then we began to laugh.

"You know," Colleen said a few minutes later (once we'd mostly, but not entirely, stopped giggling every few seconds). "Sometimes . . . I'm a little sick of being grown-up. I mean, my mom keeps saying I'm so mature with everything that happened. But I didn't know what to do." She sighed. "Sometimes I think being grown-up is overrated."

"Yeah," I said.

"Yes," Melissa said.

"Though when you had to be, you were *really* good at it," I added.

Colleen smiled. "Thanks," she said, "I'm really glad I had you guys there."

We were all quiet for a minute.

"The middle schoolers didn't seem so bad," Melissa said.

"No," I said, not hiding my surprise anymore. "They didn't."

"Yeah," Colleen agreed, nodding. "But," she went on, "don't you sort of wish . . . I mean, we're going to be middle schoolers soon, so I know we should act like it. But I actually just want to do something fun, and not worry, you know?"

I took a deep breath.

"Well," I started. "Melissa and I have been playing this game that Melissa made up. It's all about imagining there are fairies living in the field. We build houses for them, and make museums for them, and Melissa is a curating GENIUS."

"That sounds AMAZING," Colleen said. And Melissa smiled at me. A big, happy, real smile.

"Should we play fairies?" Colleen asked.

"Or museums!" Melissa said.

"Or secret agents!" I said.

"Or SUPERHEROES," Melissa said.

"*Yes*," Colleen and I cheered.

Just then, Alien-Face walked by.

"What are you doing?" he asked.

"Shhhhhhhhhh!" We (sort-of) whispered. "Get down quickly before the Villains see!"

"What?!" he said, but already in a whispery way. "Villains? Where?!"

He crouched down next to us. "Are we playing little-kid games?" he asked.

"Um, no. I've been VERY mature recently," Colleen said.

"She has," I said.

"It's really impressive," Melissa added (we're great friends this way).

"Yeah," Colleen said. "So today, we're just being ourselves."

"Superheroes!" I said.

"Superheroes!" Colleen and Melissa and Alien-Face said.

We played all recess and into the afternoon

(superheroes have secret identities after all, Ms. Clutter is proof of that. So we tried not to let on to the rest of class).

And it was really nice to be friends, and heroes, together. Friends who are there for each other always. When things are hard. And hopefully, more often than not, when things are Silly.

The next day, I went to see Ye Ye. I wanted to bring him something nice, and he can eat a lot more now, so this time, I actually went ahead with the cookie making. My mom and I made chocolate chip cookies, and Gwen helped, and Essie sat on the floor and painted all over it with the chocolate chips Gwen accidentally let her have. "Cookie, Essie," I said, looking at her happy, chocolate-mush-covered face. "Do you like cookies?"

"She loves them!" Gwen said.

"A-plus, Gwen!" I said (because grading and giving feedback is important, according to Grandma Jenkins).

My mom and I were walking down the hallway, Gwen next to me and my mom carrying Essie, when from around the corner, in Ye Ye's room, we heard familiar voices.

"WAH!" Ye Ye's voice echoed through the hallway.

"Go, go, go!" Another voice followed his, and it was—Grandpa Jenkins?

"Aaaaaaaaaaahh!!" Both voices yelled.

"What on earth is going on here?" my mom asked, as we rounded the corner and looked into the room.

"Baseball!" Grandpa Jenkins called, over Ye Ye's cheering. "Your grandmother and Nai Nai are out on a walk with Daisy, and—"

Just then the ball went flying across the TV screen.

"Gooooooooooooooo!!!!" Ye Ye and Grandpa Jenkins yelled at the same time.

"Wow," I said.

"Wow," my mom said.

"Cookie!" Gwendolyn said. (Because we'd promised her she could have one when we got inside.)

So then there were hugs, and I passed out

cookies, and Ye Ye and Grandpa Jenkins were SO happy and excited to have them. I sat with them and watched, and even though I don't know anything about baseball, they told me when to cheer, and it was a really great time.

And it was especially funny when Nai Nai and Grandma Jenkins came back, and Grandpa Jenkins said he'd take some cookies home for later, but we all saw him slip the bag under Ye Ye's pillow. I giggled, and my mom snorted, and my Nai Nai shook her head, but gave my Grandpa Jenkins a kiss on the cheek when he left.

Ye Ye was smiling and happy, and he sat up and gave me a big, real hug before I left. And from around the corner as we left, I could hear the crinkle of a cookie bag opening.

"Grandpa's really rubbing off on Ye Ye, isn't he?" I asked my mom, as we got back in the car.

"Yeah," she said, shaking her head with a smile. "Who'd have thought?"

And we made our way to the car, toward home, where there were more cookies waiting for us in the kitchen.

10

HONEY TEA

A few times, when I've been at Nai Nai and Ye Ye's, I've felt my throat get itchy and scratchy and my head start to pound.

And whenever this happens, Ye Ye makes me honey tea.

Honey tea is sweet and warm and special.

When I was little, I loved how the golden strings of honey swirled and curlicued in the hot water until they came apart and the water turned bright, golden, colorful, and clear all at the same time.

When I drank my Ye Ye's honey tea, I felt it loosen and soften the hurt feeling in my throat.

Because when you're sitting on a sofa covered in blankets, sipping something bright and sweet with your hands warm from the cup, it's hard to notice your pounding head or aches as much.

So even though, when I got older, my mom explained that honey tea is just honey mixed with hot water, not actual medicine, I didn't care.

My Ye Ye had made it just for me.

So I knew it would make me better.

I've been thinking about honey tea a lot recently. Maybe because, just a few days ago, Ye Ye finally, after what feels like FOREVER, left the hospital.

His apartment is a little different now. There are bars in the bathroom, a new special shower nozzle, and special mats for slipping. Nai Nai and

Ye Ye's bed had to be put on top of something to make it higher and easier to get into. There's a walker that he keeps by the bedroom door, and a wheelchair in the front hall closet for when he needs to go out.

I helped my dad get the changes ready (or, really, I kept him company while he looked over the shoulder of the man who was drilling everything into the wall. But that counts). Unfortunately, he also said no to some of my other suggestions for improvements, like a built-in soft-serve machine, or lights in the ceiling that projected stars on the walls, or a disco ball.

But even if my dad didn't like my (excellent) ideas, it was nice to be able to help.

And best of all, when we visited yesterday, Ye Ye was *home*.

He was tired, so we didn't stay for too long. I'd wanted to bring him balloons or throw him a party to celebrate, but my parents said no. Ye Ye's having a big birthday this summer, and my dad said we'd have a combination birthday and coming-home party then. Which is nice but made our visit less exciting than it could have been.

I sat on the couch with Ye Ye and mimed stories. And Gwen kept pulling on his leg and saying, "Ye Ye, play with me!" But Ye Ye couldn't play with her, because he couldn't sit on the floor like he used to and help put small dolls and stuffed animals in little chairs for tea parties (which used to be his and Gwen's favorite thing to do together).

And when Essie asked him to pick her up (which she does by just holding out her arms, and only every once in a while saying, "Up"), he shook his head, and Nai Nai picked her up instead.

But he did play peekaboo with Essie and make her laugh.

And when Gwen needed help with her tea party I stepped in, and we had a great time making Batman sip tea and feeding her toys dried shredded pork (which I got to eat after because it's one of my favorite snacks, so that was a win).

* * *

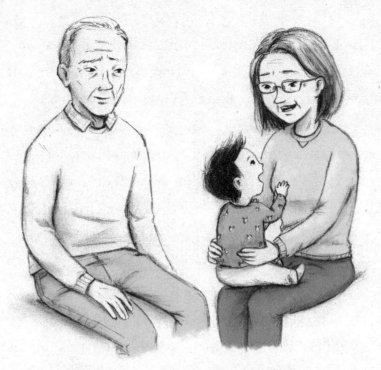

Today we didn't get to visit Ye Ye, even though
it's the weekend. My dad has a project due, and Ye
Ye has friends from Chinatown coming over. So
Nai Nai said he'd be tired out by the time we could
get there.

But we still had big plans for the day.

"So . . . ," my mom said, as we sat on the sofa
playing with blocks (in Gwen's case), eating blocks

(in Essie's case), and rolling blocks Essie's way, because it makes her laugh and maybe Gwen will see that it's fun to share (in my case).

"I was thinking," she went on, "that today might be a great day for . . . Burger Planet!"

"Burger Planet!" Gwen leaped up, scattering her blocks. "YAY!" She did a happy twirling dance (that was excellent and Very Expressive, so she's right on track Destiny-wise).

"Yay!" I said. I also love Burger Planet. Especially because even though I feel a bit too old for the Out of This World Box (which is their kids' meal, and it has a toy), I LOVE their new onion rings, and now that I don't get an Out of This World Box I'm allowed to order them. (And if someone had just told me that onions could be fried I'd probably have learned to like them A LOT sooner.)

"I want an Out of This World Box!" Gwen said, dancing up and down.

"I want onion rings!" I said, bouncing up and down.

"I want a chocolate shake!" my mom said,

picking up Gwen and dancing with her, and making her laugh, and I did the same with Essie.

We were talking and dancing around when my mom's phone rang.

"Hello," she said. Then, "Are you kidding me? On a *Saturday*?! Fine . . . sure. Look . . . I'll get it to you as soon as I can."

She hung up with a sigh.

"I'm sorry, guys. There's a crisis at work. Let me see if your dad can take you—Oh, he has his project . . ." She said some words that I'm not allowed to repeat, but they're what adults say when things are NOT working out. And I knew she was really upset.

"Don't worry, Mom," I said. "I'll watch Gwen and Essie."

"Oh . . . um . . ." She seemed to want to argue but then sighed. "Are you sure, sweetie?"

"Yeah," I said. "It'll be fun."

"THANK YOU," she said, giving me a big kiss on the forehead. "There are leftovers in the fridge for lunch."

"Great," I said.

"I'm so sorry, guys," my mom gave Gwen and Essie hugs and kisses. "I promise we'll go tomorrow. You're a lifesaver, Cilla," she said, giving me another kiss on the forehead.

I smiled, because that was really nice to hear.

My mom dashed upstairs to her office, and Gwen watched her go, with big eyes.

"I'm sorry, Gwen," I said. "It'll just be us today."

"But . . . ," she stammered. "But . . . but I want to go to Burger Planet!" Her sentence began as words but ended as a wail.

"I know." I tried to make my voice sound soothing.

"Mommy said!" Gwen started to cry.

"Yeah, she did," I said, patting her back and trying to calm her down, "but something came up."

"But . . ." Gwen's fists were curled and angry, and her cheeks were red, and I knew she was on the edge of a tantrum.

But this time, I didn't think it was annoying. Because if you're two and your mom promised you something, it must be hard to understand how the plan has to change. That's a lot to deal with, for such a small person.

In fact, it's probably really, really fuhstrating.

"But I want an Out of This World Box!" Gwen cried, and the tantrum was just a few seconds away . . .

"And you'll get one!" I said suddenly.

"I get one?" she asked, surprised.

"Yeah!" I said, getting more and more excited. "We're going to have one for lunch! It's a special kind, though, the most special of all. We're going to have it here!"

"Really?" she asked suspiciously.

"Really," I said.

"A real one?" she asked.

"Better than real," I said. "Just you wait."

I let Gwen and Essie watch a TV show while I made lunch (which is a big treat because usually TV is for the afternoons or after dinner).

I cut up carrot sticks to look just like French

fries, and I folded a piece of tin foil to look like the paper package that the French fries at Burger Planet come in. Then, with a permanent marker, I drew a giant "B" on the side of the foil, just like Burger Planet's.

For the burger, I used a roll, turkey, and slices of Gwen's favorite cheese, and I wrapped it in a piece of waxed paper, just like at Burger Planet.

For the dessert, I took out the brownies we'd had the night before, and I smooshed one into the shape of a cookie (because that's what Burger Planet gives you).

Then I found a paper bag, and drew swirls and stars all over it, and I even drew a MAZE for Gwen to complete, because the box Burger Planet gives you has games on it, and while mine wasn't quite as good as the box, I think I got pretty close.

Finally, as a finishing touch, I dashed into my room (very fast, because I know you should watch Essie at all times, but she was in front of the TV, plus this was an Emergency). I found two old toys that I hadn't played with in a loooong time—a tiny plush dog with rainbow-colored ears, and a plastic princess action figure that I'd been meaning to give away for a while.

I put the food and toys into a bag, and I crinkled up the top and rolled it shut.

I opened the front door, like someone had just knocked, and shut it again.

"Food delivery!" I said. "The Out of This World Box is here!"

"Burger Planet!" Gwen yelled.

She came running, and I met her at the living room doorway holding the bag.

"Look what they brought you, Gwen!" I said.

"Yay!!!!" she said.

"I think they even packed an extra toy for Essie!" I added.

And there was nothing for Gwen to do but her very, very happy dance.

Gwen LOVED her Out of This World Box, and Essie ate mashed peas and some crackers, and played with her new dog toy.

I sat with them, and ate leftovers, and felt a little amazed.

Because I couldn't *believe* that had worked. Gwen was SO happy, and she'd been SO sad. And somehow, I'd helped make her that way.

In fact, I felt like I'd passed a test, or proved myself in a Trial of Loyalty (which all heroes have to do at some point).

After lunch, we went to go play in the living room, and when I got down to try to grab one of Essie's toys from under the couch, I heard Gwen squeal, "Doggie pile!"

"Oh no, not the doggie pile!" I yelled in a play-scared voice.

Gwen flopped onto my back, and Essie followed.

"Oof," I said, in a non-play voice.

I sort of wished I hadn't taught them this particular trick on the one day I thought this would be the BEST way to wake my dad up from a nap (though in fairness to me it worked really well because he was VERY surprised and his face was funny to see).

But then I also laughed, because it was really funny, and Gwen and Essie were having a great time. And I propped my head on my hands, so I could turn back and make faces at them.

"Isn't this fun?!" I said, helping Essie as she scooched off my back. "Burger Planet today, and then tomorrow, we'll go see Ye Ye!"

Essie shook her head. But not in an excited way. In a way that meant "no."

"Ye Ye is boooooring," Gwen said, plopping down on the rug next to me.

"Gwen!" I gasped, shocked.

I didn't know what to say.

I wanted to explain to them that this wasn't true, and that they'd made a Terrible Mistake, but Essie started chewing on Gwen's "Out of This World toy," so suddenly there was that to deal with.

Afterward, I didn't want to talk about Ye Ye anymore. So we didn't, and luckily Gwen and Essie got really excited about making a pillow fort, which took up most of our time. We were still playing when my mom got done with her work crisis, and she gave me a big hug, and we went to the park, which was a nice end to the day. At dinner, she and my dad said they were really, really proud of me. And my mom said that later, we'd talk about starting an allowance for me, since I was such a big help.

Which was really nice.

And should feel like a victory.

But I'm not sure if it does.

*　*　*

Now, I'm in bed, thinking.

I learned a lot in these past few days. About what I can do, and about Babysitting, and taking care of people, and helping.

I'm getting so much better at it too.

But the more I learn, the more I worry that what I'm doing isn't enough.

I imagine something sweet and magic that could uncurl the stiffness in Ye Ye's smile, and bring back the strength to his arms, and unlock the words in his head.

I imagine Ye Ye, my Ye Ye, leaping out of bed like he used to jump off the couch after a nap. I imagine him spinning me and Gwen and Essie for hugs, and telling stories that make me clap, and make Gwen giggle her high laugh that sounds like a bell.

I imagine my sisters knowing Ye Ye, fun and Silly, always there for a joke, and a twirl, and a story whenever you need it.

And I remember my Epic, and how sure I was, when Ye Ye went to the hospital, that I'd make him better. That I could take care of him, and his words would come back, and everything would be the way it was before.

But sometimes, now, I wonder if that's ever really going to happen.

I wonder if Essie and Gwen will never know my fun, playing, Wise Ye Ye, who can make everything better and leap onto a carousel with one jump.

I wonder if I really am getting too old for magic.

And I wonder if I'll ever have honey tea again.

BEWARE THE PEACOCKS, AND OTHER CONCLUSIONS FROM THE ZOO

I know I haven't been the biggest fan of fifth grade. And I'm realizing that this isn't entirely fair, because there are some HUGE perks to being a fifth grader.

For example, we're having an Award Ceremony at the end of the year, complete with a pizza party for all our families. At the ceremony, there's one winner in each class for every subject. And it's the perfect opportunity, because if you win your name goes on a *plaque* in the school hallway and will *always* be there. So if you win, everyone knows that you're the best at your subject, plus your name is IMMORTAL (which is a synonym for "forever."). And I can't think of anything more Epic than that.

And, as you can probably guess, I REALLY want to win the English Award.

There are other big perks to being a fifth grader, too.

And one of these is a trip to the zoo.

I'd been looking forward to this trip all year. And there was more excitement to come, when my mom said, "Right! I signed up to help on this one— let me make sure it's in my calendar. I think I might have scheduled a meeting then."

"Oh, a field trip?" my dad said. "I'll go."

"It's okay, Nathan," my mom said, flipping through her calendar. I'm sure I can reschedule. I know things are hectic . . ."

"No, seriously," my dad said. "I know I haven't been around much—with everything going on—and we're long overdue for some quality time together. Right, kiddo?" he asked, mussing my hair.

"Yeah!" I said. "Plus there are supposed to be

PEACOCKS there, and you can meet Mimi Donnelly and tell me if you think she's to be trusted."

"See?" He turned to my mom with a laugh. "I have a lot to do."

There was nothing for my mom to do but laugh too and say, "You win!"

So then my dad leaned over and kissed her, and I looked away and said, "GROSSSSSS," and held up my hand to block them out, because that's what Colleen does with her parents.

But secretly, it made me kind of happy.

And ESPECIALLY because my DAD was coming to the ZOO.

The day of the field trip arrived. My dad drove me to school, and he and I packed lunches in brown paper bags.

("Burger Planet?" Gwen asked when she saw them.

"No," I said. "These are just normal lunches. But we'll have to get delivery from them again soon."

"Yeah!" she said.)

It was funny to have my dad in school with me, and to see other parents in school. Tim #2's step-mom was there, and so was Melissa's dad, and Melvin's mom.

Ms. Paradise had asked all the chaperones to take pictures during the day, so my dad had brought his big and fancy camera, which was his birthday gift from my mom last year.

We all rode a bus to the zoo (which was also funny, because it's always weird to be on a school bus and to realize that one of your parents is sitting in the front seat, telling jokes with Melissa's dad).

Before we left, Ms. Paradise divided us all into groups. Sadly, Colleen was in a group with Ms. Paradise as a chaperone, and Melissa was with her dad (which makes sense, but still was sad, because it would have been fun to go around the zoo with her, and Colleen should have DEFINITELY been in my group because we're best friends).

But, at least Alien-Face was with me. So was

Tim #1 (which made Alien-Face smile), then Lina, Sally, and, last of all, *Mimi Donnelly.*

Which was funny because this time I was actually glad, because my dad would get a chance to see her all day and tell me what he thought.

The zoo was possibly the best place I've ever visited. There were peacocks and baby ducks wandering around, not in cages. We saw panda bears in big enclosures full of beautiful green leaves and trees, and one panda sat on a branch and watched us as it chewed a stick, and I imagined SO MANY stories about what it was thinking. We also went inside a butterfly house, a building made of clear glass where there are plants and butterflies EVERY-WHERE. They flew around us, we held out honey treats for them, a butterfly landed on Tim #1's NOSE and on my shoulder, and my dad got pictures both times and it was MAGICAL. We also saw a hippo BABY, which was tiny compared to the parents but actually HUGE, and it lay with its face half in the water and blinked sleepily and blew bubbles.

There were other highlights of the day too.

And one of the best came at lunchtime.

Our group had gathered around one long picnic table, and everyone was pulling out their lunches and bags of food. I had just taken a bite of my sandwich, when I heard Alien-Face yell.

"Look," he said, "a peacock!"

"Wow," I said. It was *right in front of us*, strutting up and down the rows of picnic tables, its beautiful blue and purple feathers ruffled out in a shining fan.

"Get a picture, Mr. Lee," Mimi said.

I heard the camera go "Click! Click! Click!"

"Do you think it lives here all the time?" Alien-Face asked me, as the peacock came closer and the camera clicked away.

"I don't know," I said. "I think so—Aaaah!"

My sandwich was suddenly GONE.

Specifically, into the beak of the peacock, which had suddenly, without warning, darted forward and grabbed it. The peacock who was now shuffling away, with my lunch in its mouth.

I heard my tablemates shouting, and my dad saying, "Are you okay, Cilla?!"

I'd jumped up before I really realized that I probably did NOT want my sandwich back from the peacock's mouth.

The funny part was, the peacock knew it too. It didn't run away or anything. Instead, it turned back to look at me, totally unconcerned. Then it dropped *my* sandwich on the ground, picked out the pieces of bread, and started waddling away with them, just as calmly as it had walked into the pavilion. But suddenly—

I gasped, as I realized what lay in front of me. It had fallen from the peacock's tail, right at my feet. I picked it up. It was a long and perfect peacock feather—purple, blue, and green.

"Thank you!" I shouted after the peacock. "Enjoy the sandwich!"

Because even though I was hungry, that seemed like more than a fair trade.

Melissa's dad watched our group while my dad took me to buy a new lunch and to wash my hands.

He said I could keep the feather, but apparently we had to disinfect it before I could really play with it. Which makes no sense because it was VERY clean—how else could it be so bright and colorful? But he insisted, and I knew there was no fighting it.

"Wow," my dad said once we were in line (with clean hands). "What an Adventure."

"Seriously!" I said. "I can't wait to tell mom about it!"

"I was taking a picture right as it happened," he said. "I think I actually got a photo. Let's look." He showed me the screen on the camera; we scrolled through.

There was a photo of me and Alien-Face laughing, and the peacock just behind us.

And then—

"You got it, Dad!" I yelled.

There, on the screen, was a picture of the *exact* moment that it happened. A picture of me, my mouth wide in shock, as the peacock pulled my sandwich out of my hands.

"That is the best thing I have EVER SEEN," I said,

when we'd caught our breath from laughing. And to be fair, I really wasn't exaggerating—how often do you get to meet a robber peacock, let alone catch it *on camera*?!

The line for food was a little long, but luckily we were too busy laughing over the photos to notice. Then my dad showed me the others he'd taken that day.

"These are amazing!" I said.

"Thanks," he said, smiling. "I wanted to be a photographer when I was younger, you know. I was always making art when I was little, and in high school I even got a scholarship to an arts school. That's why your mom got me this camera."

"Wow," I said. I hadn't known that. "Why didn't you go?"

"Because of Nai Nai and Ye Ye," Dad said. "They were very Traditional Chinese parents. So they said no."

"But—" I looked up at him. "But why would they do that? I mean, why would they . . . ?"

"Sweetie, it's nothing to get upset about," he

said. "They were just trying to take care of me. Things were very hard for them when they first came here. They wanted me to be okay, and to have a job, and enough money to have a family, and to them, the way to get all that was to go into a certain kind of work."

I'd sort of known this about Nai Nai and Ye Ye. But I hadn't realized that it actually meant that my dad couldn't do things he'd really wanted to do.

"It's okay, sweetheart," he said, taking my hand. "I split the difference and became a graphic designer, which meant I got to do art, but I also have a more traditional job. That's why I started my own business. It means I can do more of the art I want to, and go back to all the things I loved when I was a kid."

"Oh," I said. I didn't know you could do that.

Then, something else occurred to me.

"But . . . Nai Nai and Ye Ye know I want to be a writer, and they've never told me to do something else. They buy me notebooks, and they love my stories."

"Yeah," he said, "and it's great. They've changed as they've gotten older. They're much more laid-back. And they want you to be happy."

"Huh," I said. This was a nice idea.

"Is this why you never taught us Chinese?" I asked.

"Um . . ." He made a thinking face. "I've never thought about it. I dunno. I think I just wanted to leave some of those old ways and expectations behind. And since your mom doesn't know any Chinese, it made it even easier to do that. Why?" he asked. "Do you want to learn?"

"I mean"—I shrugged—"sometimes I think it would be nice. Especially with Ye Ye."

"Well," my dad said. "We can look into that. Maybe we can find you some Cantonese classes over the summer."

"Yeah!" I said with a big smile. "And maybe you can find a photography class."

"Uh, I don't need a photography class," my dad teased. "I'll have you know that I'm an excellent artist."

"Well, I am too, and—" I began to tease back. But then something else occurred to me. "Wait, Dad," I gasped. "Do you know what this means?!"

"Um, what?"

"You have your own Epic destiny! It runs in the family! And now," I went on, "you have someone to believe in you, because I do, and I bet Nai Nai and Ye Ye do too, now that you're older, and Mom, because she bought you the camera. So you should take more photos, Dad! You have to cultivate your art. You can't fight destiny. It's never too late!"

My dad laughed, and people around us in line looked at me a little funny, because I was maybe VERY carried away. But I didn't mind. Because this is Destiny we were talking about. And Destiny is Serious Business.

"Well, thank you, Cilla," my dad said. "You know"—his voice was more Serious now—"you're right. I should start taking more photos, even if it's not for work. I really do love it."

"Excellent," I said as we neared the food counter. "Also, when you're a famous photographer and everyone's giving you money to take their photo, remember who got you started."

My dad laughed as the clerk called us forward. "So you're asking if you can have fries *and* a soda?"

"Yes." I grinned, because he knows me very well.

"Sure," he said, grinning back. "But don't tell your mom."

We both got sodas, and I got French fries and a hot dog to replace my sandwich, and it was a fun time.

And as if all this wasn't enough Drama and excitement, and as if I hadn't already learned SO MUCH about my dad, I learned EVEN MORE before the day was done.

Because after lunch came the exhibit that Alien-Face and Mimi were the most excited about— the exhibit called BIG CATS! (This isn't just me being Dramatic—that's what the sign says. The letters are all caps and streaked with tiger stripes, and the exclamation mark is dotted with a giant cat pawprint.)

The first stop was the tiger enclosure. It was a

bright, sunny day, so the tigers were in their outside cage, separated from us by two layers of wire. But there wasn't glass or anything, which was exciting, because as Alien-Face pointed out, we and the tigers were breathing the same air.

"Okay, guys, get in front of the wire," my dad said, raising his camera. "One, two, achoo!!" The click went off, but the camera had moved with his sneeze. "Sorry!" he said. "One, two, thr—AaaaCHOOO!"

"Sorry!" my dad said again, shaking his head. "Must be the pollen."

"Here, Dad!" I ran over to him. "I can take them. It'll be fun!"

"Thanks, sweetie," he said, as he wiped his nose with a tissue from his pocket.

"Click." I took a photo of Alien-Face waving at one of the tigers.

"Click." Mimi wanted a photo where she was scared of the tiger, and then another where she was roaring at it (which was all very impressive, and I hoped my dad was paying attention, because imagination is a good thing to judge someone on).

All the while—"Achoo!!" my dad said. He went over by the cage to get out of the way of a family with a stroller. "Achoo!" he said again. I took a photo.

The tiger, in the background, came closer to the wire.

"Ah-Ah-CHOO!!!!"

"Click." The camera caught it, and I was very pleased with the photo I'd taken, my dad sneezing, a GIANT tiger in the background, crouching, looking just like the exhibit said, a—

"DAD!" I said suddenly. "Your allergies."

"Wha-ACHOO!" he tried to ask.

"You know how you're allergic to cats?" I said. "Well . . ."

My dad turned to look at the tiger, which was looking at him through the chain-link.

"I mean, it *is* a BIG cat," I said.

"Ha, ha-aaacho!" my dad said, laughing and sneezing all at once, and it was impressive, and I took a picture.

"I think you're right, kiddo," he said. "Um, guys,

I'm just going to stand over here . . . ," he said, moving away from the fences.

"WOW," Alien-Face whispered as he went. "That is the BEST problem to have."

We had a great day at the zoo. And on the way back to school, when we were all tired and smelled of sunblock, we talked about our trip and compared all the things our groups had done and seen.

"Our group had the BEST time," Tim #2 said. "A flamingo *splashed* me."

"Oh yeah?" Colleen said. "Well, I saw a giraffe *running*. It picked a leaf from a tree and chewed it right in front of me."

"Well, I got a feather in a deal with a peacock," I said, pointing to the feather poking up from the front of the bus (my dad was holding it for safe-keeping).

"Yeah." Mimi nodded in agreement. "Plus, her dad's allergic to TIGERS. Which is EPIC."

"*Whoa*," Tim #2 said.

"*Wow,*" Colleen said.

"That's *amazing,*" Melissa and Sally said.

"Yeah." I smiled at Mimi. "And that."

Our day at the zoo gave me SO MANY ideas for new stories (because tigers, peacock robberies, and fun times with your dad are all *great* material for Adventures). But it gave me something else too. That day, I decided to give Mimi Donnelly another chance. Because I'm learning that, actually, everyone has a story. In fact, everyone has lots of stories. My dad is my dad, but also a son. He's an artist too, and someone who's going back to his art, back to what he loved as a kid, after a long time. Which is really, really brave.

And Ye Ye and Nai Nai are my Ye Ye and Nai Nai, who love me and support me in all the things I do. But they also are a dad and a mom, who didn't make all the right decisions, and didn't always know the right ways to Take Care. But they've changed now, and that's a really impressive story too.

And Mimi Donnelly is a younger sister, and she worries about what other people think about her, like me. She was mean to me because she was worried about what Lisa thought. And that wasn't right. But I know how that feels—I hurt Melissa's feelings because I was worried too. Even Lisa probably has a story, and a reason why she thinks she has to be mean to people (not that I like her or ever will. But it's still nice to know).

And I knew, as I smiled at Mimi as we got off the bus, that I'd made the right choice.

Besides, anyone who can appreciate a good Epic is okay in my book.

TIMELESSNESS

One of the best parts of visiting with Ms. Clutter (other than hearing her funny jokes and trying to guess her superhero powers) is getting to talk about books.

We talk about the stories we like, and the stories that don't quite work for us. We talk about the stories that are predictable, but it's okay because they're still entertaining; and the stories that, once you realize what's going to happen, aren't fun anymore.

Now, whenever I read a new book and it reminds me of another book I love, I add it to the lists that Ms. Clutter and I keep. And every few weeks she prints out a new "If you liked" list, and it's really nice to see *my* ideas there, printed on an official piece of paper for ALL the school to see.

And Ms. Clutter will tell me when a student comes in and says they liked a recommendation I suggested. Which makes me feel very proud.

One of the big ideas Ms. Clutter and I have been talking about recently is something called Time-lessness.

A Timeless story is a story that everyone can enjoy and understand, no matter when or where it was written.

Timelessness is great to talk about, because it's the kind of story an Epic is, since Struggles, Triumphs, Drama, and dragons have been around for FOREVER, and I can't imagine that people will stop enjoying them.

But there's an opposite of timeless too. This is when you're something my mom calls "a product of your time."

And I'm sorry to say that when my mom says this, she's always talking about my Grandpa Jenkins.

"Being a product of your time" is everything but Timeless. It means that you have a hard time with new things.

So when I noticed that, at dinner, everyone helps, and cooks, and clears, except for my Grandpa Jenkins, my mom explained that Grandpa Jenkins grew up in a different time from ours, when dads didn't really help with the housework, or with kids.

Once she pointed this out, I started noticing it more and more. Grandpa Jenkins never changes any of Essie's diapers. And when Essie spits up, he wrinkles his nose and says, "Delightful," in a kind of voice that means it's the opposite of delightful, and hands her to someone else. And when Gwen makes a mess or starts to cry, he doesn't know what to do.

My mom says that it all works out because Grandma and Grandpa Jenkins have an Arrangement that works for them, but that it's really different from what she and my dad do.

The more Independent I get, the more I see this. I see how it makes a BIG difference. When my Grandma Jenkins makes dinner, she's not just thinking about dinner. In the morning she has to know what's in the refrigerator, she has to plan if she's going to the grocery store, she has to know what dishes are in the wash, when to clean and get things ready, and on top of that she has to remember to always check Essie's diapers and to give Gwen snacks. Having me around helps a lot, of course. But the more I do, the more I notice all the things she has to keep in her head. And Grandpa Jenkins helps, but it's a different kind, and his head is free for other things, because he's never thinking about things like the groceries, or cleaning, or food, or spit-up.

It's different at home. Because even though my mom and dad have different ways of doing things, and my mom always adds salt to the soups my dad makes when he's not looking, and my dad sighs when my mom dusts because she's missing the corners, they're both still doing work. And if my mom's having a bad day, my dad will call her and say, "Don't worry about a thing," and he knows that there's A LOT involved in making her not worry: there's the dinner to make, and kitchen to clean, and lunches to make for the next day, and the hamper to check, and bath times, and home-work help for me. But he knows all this, just like she knows all this, and they both do it.

Usually, I don't really think about the fact that my Grandpa Jenkins is a product of his time. It's just the way things are.

But sometimes, it's hard to avoid.

Which is what happened this morning.

I woke up for school today excited for band, and I tried to say good morning to my mom.

But the sound was all croaky and didn't feel good coming from my throat. My mom frowned.

"Are you feeling okay?" she asked.

"Yes," I croaked, hoping it was true. I didn't want to miss practicing our new song.

My mom rested her hand on my forehead, which felt soft and cool, and I realized maybe I did feel funny.

"I think you have a fever," she said.

I did, and it's the flu, and it was all ESPECIALLY awful, because usually being sick can feel like a fun treat, even if you don't feel that great, because you get to stay home and lie on the couch and watch cartoons during the day.

But I wanted to go to band—we only have a few more music classes left, with the school year almost over. So I want to enjoy band as much as I can now (especially since I don't know if middle school band will be as fun, or if even more people there will make fun of me for playing the tuba).

Then, on top of that, I found out that being sick means I won't be able to visit Ye Ye for AT LEAST a week, because you have to make sure you're done being sick so he doesn't catch anything, and that was AWFUL.

And to make everything worse, my mom had a really important meeting, and my dad had to meet a big client, and Nai Nai was running errands for Ye Ye, and Grandma Jenkins had a class to teach.

Which is how it happened that my Grandpa Jenkins came over to stay with me.

At first, I tried to fight this. "I can stay home by myself," I said. "It's only for the morning." But my mom said no. More specifically, "Are you kidding?! Not a chance, Young Lady" (which is a very Extreme form of no, so you know she's Serious).

"Well," I said (or, really, croaked), "what if he just comes to check on me? I can take care of myself."

But the answer was also no.

So then I tried to explain the real problem.

"But, Mom," I said. "What will we do? Grandpa Jenkins doesn't know how to make Popsicles, or soup, or take temperatures, and he won't like it, and—"

"It will be fine, sweetheart," my mom said, patting my hair and giving me a kiss on my forehead. "I'll tell him exactly what to do, I promise." When she says things like this it usually does make me feel better, but somehow, it didn't just then.

Grandpa Jenkins came over soon after that, and he brought me a book with puzzles in it, and a little plastic horse figurine to play with, which was very nice of him. My mom made me a bed on the couch, and in the other room, I could hear her telling Grandpa Jenkins all about the soup cans she was leaving out—all he had to do was heat them.

While I heard all of this, I felt a bad rumbling in my stomach, but I didn't say anything. I didn't want my mom to miss her meeting, but most of all, I didn't want my Grandpa Jenkins to say "delightful" in that voice that means something other than what he's actually saying. So when my mom came over and asked, "Everything okay?" I said yes. And even though she frowned for a minute like she didn't believe me, she said, "Okay," and "I love you," and she gave me a hug and a kiss and reminded me to call if I needed her, and said, "Thanks again, Dad, you're a lifesaver." She grabbed her briefcase and ran out the door.

"Well, Cilla, my dear," Grandpa Jenkins said, coming to sit in the chair next to me. "It's just you and me. What would you like to do?"

"Can we watch TV?" I asked in a small voice, trying to ignore the way my stomach felt.

"Of course," he said.

We found a cartoon station that I liked, and I said, "I'm okay. You can sit in the other room and do your crossword, if you want" (because he loves crosswords).

"Well, I'll stay here," he said. But he did pull out his crossword, and we sat there for a while like that, and I hoped the TV sounds weren't bothering him. And even though I liked the cartoon show we'd found (the mice always do a dance after they've saved the world from evil, and there are some GREAT car chases), I couldn't focus, because my head hurt and I can't see Ye Ye for a week, and my Grandpa Jenkins didn't think it was his job to take care of kids, and my throat was sore and my stomach, and . . .

Grandpa Jenkins was saying something to me, but I wasn't sure what, when I jumped up from the couch and ran to the bathroom, and started to be maybe a little bit sick. And it didn't feel good, and my nose was stuffy, and I could feel my eyes hot and crying a little, and would my Grandpa Jenkins wrinkle his nose and think I was gross, and where was my mom, and—

"Shhh, it's okay." I felt cool hands softly pulling my hair away from my forehead. "It's okay, Cilla, I'm here," my Grandpa said, rubbing my back. "Get it out, I'll sit with you until it's over."

"You . . . ," I said, sniffing, "you don't have to. I'm okay."

"Don't be Silly," he said, in a nice, calm-sounding voice, rubbing my back with his hand. "Of course I won't leave you."

"Oh," I said.

When I was done being sick (which I'll admit, was more than a little gross), Grandpa Jenkins took a washcloth and helped me wash my face and hands. Then he patted me dry and carried me back to the couch, which I didn't even know he could do, it's been so long since he's carried me.

He tucked me in and showed me a trick where you tuck the blankets underneath the couch cushions to make them snug and tight, which felt nice and made me giggle, because he has A LOT of opinions on how to tuck in sheets and make a bed Just Right.

Grandpa Jenkins sat down, but didn't take out his crossword this time. "Now," he said, "what's happening here? Dancing mice, huh?" So I explained how they only dance after they've saved the world, and we watched a whole two more episodes, and when the bad guy came on-screen, Grandpa Jenkins gasped and agreed that he was pretty scary (he has the head of a lion, after all).

And I was impressed.

"Grandpa," I said, a little later, after I was feeling much better and sort of sitting up and playing a game of Go Fish, "you're really good at taking care of kids."

"Why, thank you, Cilla," he said. "That means a lot."

"It's just," I said again, after a minute, "I thought you didn't know how."

"Well," he said, putting down another Go Fish card. "I never did, really, until you came along, and then your cousin, Helen, and now Gwen and Essie. I grew up in a different time. It never really occurred to me that I could stay home with the kids—I was always working. Why, I was even working the night your mother was born. Fathers weren't allowed in hospital rooms then, to be with their wives. I had a big deal to close, too, so I stayed at work until it was all over."

"Wow," I said.

"Pretty bad, right?" he said with a small laugh. "Luckily, things have changed. I'm glad, because I've learned new things as time's gone on. It's a good thing, too, because if I hadn't, I'd miss out on afternoons like this, with my favorite oldest granddaughter."

He smiled, and I smiled, and then I said, "Go Fish."

A little while later, my Grandpa Jenkins said I should put something in my stomach. He brought me a plate of crackers, which I ate slowly as I watched another cartoon. So I was barely paying attention when Grandpa Jenkins put a cup of something hot in my hands.

I took a sip and almost dropped the cup in surprise.

"Honey tea!" I said.

"Your Ye Ye told me you liked it," he said, "and how to make it. Well, he told me, and your Nai Nai translated. He has VERY specific ideas about how much honey to add, and the right way to stir. We should call later today, when your Nai Nai's there. You can tell them how you're feeling. I know he'll be worried."

Grandpa Jenkins put his hand on my forehead as I leaned back into the cushions, holding my steaming mug. His hand felt nice and cool, and I closed my eyes and took a sip of my tea, and breathed in the familiar steam.

And my honey tea, made for me by Grandpa

Jenkins and my Ye Ye, was just like it's always been: sweet, and warm, and magic.

I sipped my honey tea, as the hurt in my throat softened, and listened to the sounds of my Grandpa Jenkins dropping things in the kitchen while he made me soup (it's okay—he's trying. Just give him time).

And I felt a lot better.

My dad came home soon after that, and he said I was looking much better, though I probably still would need to stay home from school tomorrow, just in case. But my Grandpa said he'd come to keep me company in the afternoon again, and promised to teach me a game called backgammon, which he used to play with his grandmother, and which sounds very exciting.

Right now, I'm writing this chapter from the white-and-blue-striped living room couch. I am eleven and a half years old, the sky outside is sunny, the flowers are just beginning to blossom, and today is a sick day. But none of these details actually matter.

Because this story, like my Grandpa Jenkins, is timeless.

GRADUATIONS

A Graduation marks a big change.

So I guess it makes sense that there's been A LOT of big changes recently.

It's just that time.

The morning of the fifth-grade graduation ceremony, my mom helped me get ready and drove me to school, where the rest of my family would meet me later.

"Are you excited, sweetie?" she asked.

"Yeah," I said quietly. "It'll be fun." And I was excited, even though the idea of all those people, and English Awards, and the last day of elementary school, made my stomach a little fluttery. "Mimi

Donnelly will win the English Award, though," I said, after a moment.

"So?" my mom asked. "Even if that's true, it's still your day. Award or no, you have so much to be proud of." She gave me a hug.

"Yeah," I said.

Because I knew it was true.

But I still wanted it.

I thought about this conversation as my classmates and I took our seats and turned with everyone else to try to find our families in the auditorium behind us.

"I see Ye Ye!" Alien-Face yelled. We both began to wave as he pointed me to the middle row, where Ye Ye sat between Nai Nai and Grandpa Jenkins. Next to them, my mom, dad, Gwen, Essie, and Grandma Jenkins sat, talking and laughing with Colleen's family in the row in front of them.

I was just turning back from my waving, when I heard a voice say my name. A voice I didn't know that well but which was familiar all the same.

"Cilla!" I turned. There, standing right at the edge of my row, was *Hattie Donnelly*. "You're Cilla, right?" she asked, leaning over Alien-Face.

"Um, yeah," I said, sitting up straight and trying to be very calm and Serious.

"I'm sorry, I know I shouldn't be bugging you before the ceremony," she said, "but Mimi just told me you play the tuba! *I* play the tuba!"

"WHAT?!" I said (maybe forgetting about Seriousness for a minute).

"Yeah!" she said, jumping up and down with a grin that was big like mine. "I'm the section leader next year! It's going to be SO AMAZING having another girl in the brass section. And we're going to be getting a new teacher too. He used to teach band at the high school, and my older brother says he's a real ogre, but then when you get to know him he's really nice. So don't worry, we'll face him together! Brass Buddies for Life!" she said, punching the air, in a way that was VERY Dramatic, and not Serious, and great.

"Yeah!" I said, punching the air too. "Brass Buddies for Life!"

And then Dr. Torres, our principal, cleared her throat and said, "Let's settle down now," so Hattie had to go back to her seat. But she waved and smiled and said, "We'll talk soon!"

The ceremony began. One student from each class won each award, and they went up to the stage to shake hands with Dr. Torres and the teacher giving the award, and they got a certificate to hang on their wall that said their name in fancy gold letters.

Mr. Pod announced the Science Award, and I held my breath, and Colleen WON! There was A LOT of cheering (though I, Alien-Face, and Melissa were the loudest, of course). Especially when Mr. Pod said he was sure she'd make it to space someday, when he shook her hand.

Melissa won the Art Award, and Alien-Face and a beaming Colleen and I yelled her name as loud as we could. And Alien-Face got a special Citizen's

Award, for being a great member of the community, and I was REALLY happy for him because he is.

Finally, last of all, it was time for the English Award.

"The English Award goes to students who have demonstrated excellence in their writing, and who have shown creativity, dedication, and passion for the art of writing," Ms. Sutter, the fifth-grade English tutor, said, reading from a card. "From Mr. Kessler's class, the English Award goes to Billy Lane!" Everyone cheered, and I did too, because Billy's very nice. "From Ms. Glazer's class, the award goes to Yasmin Aguilar!" We all cheered because Yasmin is great and tells AMAZING stories. "Finally, from Ms. Paradise's class, the English Award goes to . . ."

I held my breath.

"Mimi Donnelly!"

There was applause, and I saw Mimi get up with a giant smile on her face to join the others onstage.

I felt disappointed, and my breath came out in a sad kind of sigh.

But I realized that my hands were clapping too, along with everyone else.

And I saw what my mom meant about Changes, and how this was a time of big and unexpected ones.

Because I was sad. I'd really wanted that award.

But I saw Mimi's smile, and I heard her family (and Hattie!) cheering. And I felt *happy* for her.

Which was weird.

But nice.

The winners made their way back to their seats,

and we waited for Dr. Torres to come up and finish the assembly.

But I looked away for a minute, so I could smile and give Mimi a thumbs-up as she sat down, and she smiled and waved back at me.

So I didn't notice who the next speaker was, until I heard a familiar voice begin to speak.

"Hello," the voice said. "Usually the English Award is the last award given out to our students. But this year, I'm delighted to announce a new award, in a category we've never given out before."

I looked up. There, at the podium, was *Ms. Clutter*.

"The brand-new Library Award," she went on, "will be awarded to one student from the whole fifth grade who shows outstanding commitment to our library, and to reading. This year, our very first winner is someone who has truly made a difference to our reading community. She's visited the library almost every day since the school year began. She's volunteered her time to help create reading lists and book recommendations. And she's always willing to try a new book and help a fellow classmate find a good story. So, the Library Award this year, for the very first time, goes to—"

Colleen was already nudging me, but I could barely make sense of what was happening and—

"Cilla Lee-Jenkins!" Ms. Clutter finished.

All around me my friends and classmates began to clap, and I heard Colleen yelling my name and Alien-Face and Melissa. But I also heard Mimi saying, "WOW, CILLA!" And from the middle of the audience, I heard the unmistakable sound of my family, cheering.

"I'm so proud of you, Cilla!" Ms. Clutter said, as she gave me a BIG hug and handed me a certificate, written in fancy gold letters, in a gold frame.

"Thank you, Ms. Clutter!" I said, as she put her arm around me and turned me so I could hold up my certificate.

And that moment, with my Ye Ye *standing* as he clapped, Grandpa Jenkins with his arm around Ye Ye, holding Gwen with the other and cheering, my Nai Nai and Grandma Jenkins leaning against each other as they clapped and yelled, my mom

clapping her hands with shiny eyes as she held
Gwendolyn, and above it all the unmistakable
"click" and flashing of my dad's camera, felt like
something Epic all its own.

I walked my family to our classroom for our
class party, and Ye Ye and I exchanged special, in-
joke looks as we went. (When he saw the pineapples
he raised his eyebrows and gave me a glance that
meant "Oh my goodness, it IS A Bit Much.")

All our families were there, and everyone was
talking excitedly.

"Cilla!" Colleen yelled, running over and jump-
ing up and down, as she looked at my award and
I admired the gold-lined planet drawn on hers.
"You're the first-ever Library Award winner, Cilla!
They MADE IT FOR YOU!" she said.

"Well, Mr. Pod said you're DEFINITELY going
to space," I said, also hopping up and down.

"Best day ever!" she said, throwing her arms
around me.

"Oh, now smile!" I heard my dad's voice call out above all the talking and laughing around us.

So we did, and my dad took a photo and showed it to us on the view screen.

"Beautiful, Dad!" I said.

Because feedback is important.

Besides, he's a VERY talented photographer, which I know because he'd caught the perfect moment.

Which makes sense. It's his Destiny, after all.

My dad had a chance to capture LOTS more perfect moments that afternoon.

There was the picture of Ye Ye and Alien-Face, each with their mouths wide-open, about to bite into GIANT pieces of pizza. There was a picture of me, Melissa, and her Abuela, holding up Melissa's Art Award. There was a picture of me, Nai Nai, Ye Ye, Grandma Jenkins, Grandpa Jenkins, and Essie and Gwen, with Gwen clutching my Library Award and Essie trying to chew the corner. (Don't worry, Grandma Jenkins stopped her juuuust in time.) There was a picture of me, Hattie, and Mimi smiling.

There was even a picture of me, Ms. Clutter, and Ms. Paradise.

And if you'd heard our conversation just before my dad took that photo, you might have been surprised. Because Mrs. Paradise had made her way through all the families, talking and laughing, to find me.

"Congratulations, Cilla!" she said. "I was thrilled when Ms. Clutter suggested this. She and I went to Dr. Torres together and convinced her that she HAD to make this new award. The plaque will be here soon, and your name will be the first one on it!"

"Wow," I said. "Thank you, Ms. Paradise!"

I felt a smile grow on my face, and Ms. Paradise grinned back.

Just then, Ms. Clutter walked over, and my dad said, "Smile!" So we did.

And as the camera clicked, I realized that maybe fifth grade wasn't a paradise. But Ms. Paradise hadn't been that bad, either.

She may have even been a Wise Guide, kind of like Ms. Clutter.

Though without the same amazing style, and probably without the superpowers, too.

At the end of the party, Ms. Paradise gave a speech.

"Coming to a new school, and teaching a new grade hasn't been easy," she said. "But this class has been everything I could hope for: generous to me and understanding of my mistakes—"

("Oops," Colleen whispered with a guilty smile. I grinned sheepishly and agreed.)

"—fun, excited to learn," Ms. Paradise went on. "Above all, they've cared for each other and supported each other in ways that never fail to surprise and impress me. Thank you to my fifth graders," she said, raising her cup of juice in a toast. "The middle school is lucky to have you."

All the parents said, "Hear! Hear!"

Colleen and I looked at each other.

"Maybe we should come back to visit," I whispered.

"Yeah," she whispered. "I mean she's new to the school, so she doesn't know a lot of kids. We can't abandon her."

"Yeah." I nodded. "Exactly."

* * *

The day wound down, and soon all our parents were packing up.

Hattie left with her parents, carrying some of Mimi's notebooks. But right before she left, she came dashing over to me.

"I came up with the perfect name for us next year! Operation Overcome Ogre!"

"Yes!" I gasped. "And our tubas will be our Magic Talismans, protecting us!"

"YES!" she said, jumping up and down. Then her parents called, and she raced away to catch up with them.

I watched her go, and Colleen and I exchanged surprised but happy glances.

And all I could do was grin.

Because Operation Overcome Ogre was a great story. An EPIC one.

And in middle school, of all places.

As we packed up our desks, I looked up for a moment and watched my family as Nai Nai and Grandpa Jenkins helped Ye Ye make his way toward the classroom door.

I held my award and looked at it, and at Mimi Donnelly, with the English Award that I'd wanted so badly.

And I saw the story I'd had in my head. The one that said I *had* to get that award.

That story hadn't come true. But it was okay that it hadn't.

And I'd told myself that middle school was where my stories would have to stop. But actually, that's not true. My Epic Adventure gets to keep going.

As I watched my family, I realized that I had another story in my head too.

A story about Ye Ye.

A story that also isn't true.

Because Ye Ye isn't going to get his English back right now. Maybe not even ever.

I've known this for a while.

But it's a hard story to change.

I felt sad as I watched my Ye Ye go, and let the story go with him.

I clutched my Library Award, and I thought of

the unexpected things that happen, outside of any story you can imagine or make up. And how some of them can be really, really nice and not bad things at all.

And as I walked with my classmates out the doorway of Ms. Paradise's classroom, and for the last time, down the hallway of our elementary school, with the other classes lined up to see us off, and cheering, it happened.

As one story left, another one came.

Something new and unexpected,

Something Silly and Serious all at the same time,

Something Epic.

THE EPIC OF CILLA LEE-JENKINS

On the day of my Ye Ye's birthday and coming- home party, I wore my red-and-gold cheongsam, which is a beautiful Chinese dress.

I had the perfect gift for him, too.

Banquets have SO MUCH food. You sit at round tables, and each has a spinning tray in the middle that moves the food around and around (and closer and closer to you, which is maybe the most important part). There are so many courses too, and it feels impossible to keep track. There was duck, shrimp, sizzling tofu, noodles, scallop soup, spare ribs, soy-sauce chicken, bok choy, and so much more. Plus my Ye Ye made sure that there would also be tzuck sang there too. Just for me. And for Nai Nai. Because we have a favorite food in common, which is possibly the best kind of Similarity there is.

The restaurant was big and bustling. Everywhere I looked were my family and friends. Aunties and Uncles from Chinatown and the community center laughed and joked, and Ronnie from the hospital sat at their table, laughing along with them. Auntie Eva sat talking and laughing with my mom, her arm resting on her stomach (another GIANT surprise), which was big, and round, and smooth.

My dad threw Gwen into the air while she shrieked and laughed and said, "Again, Daddy, again!" Essie sat with Nai Nai and Uncle Paul (Auntie Eva's husband) and nibbled on something she was clearly enjoying—her first taste of snails. (Trust me, they're delicious.)

My Grandma Jenkins sat with Ye Ye, and Ye Ye was already wearing Grandpa Jenkins's gift for him—a bow tie with the logo of their favorite baseball team.

Everyone was talking, and laughing, and happy.

And I was too.

Especially when it was time for presents.

"Happy birthday, Ye Ye," I said. I had to lay the gift down on the table, because it was big, and I worried he wouldn't be able to hold the whole thing.

He put his hand to his chest with a surprised smile as if to say, "For me?!"

I nodded, and smiled back.

It took him a minute to tear off the paper. But he did it, with both hands, slowly and carefully. Finally, he peeled back the gold layer.

"Ay yah!" he said.

That seemed to be all he could say, for a minute. And then, "BEAUTIFUL," he said in a happy whisper.

And it was (if I do say so myself).

The photo was the size of a small poster, and safely behind glass in a beautiful frame that I'd bought with my brand-new allowance (plus a little help from my dad, because he said it was a Special Occasion so we should only get the Best. And a brand-new middle school allowance apparently doesn't quite cover the Best. But we'll get there).

In the photo, I wore the very same cheongsam I was wearing now. I lay on my stomach in front of a white wall, smiling at the camera. And above me, Gwen and Essie were happily dog-piled across on my back, both wearing their cheongsams too. In her hands, Essie held a baseball out to the camera, like she was just about to throw it (which she actually did a moment later—my dad took the photo just in time). And on our heads, we all wore baseball caps, bright with the logo of my Ye Ye and Grandpa Jenkins's favorite team.

"Guess who took it, Ye Ye?" I asked.

But I didn't even need to tell him.

"Wah"—he turned to my dad—"what an artist!"

He reached out a hand and squeezed my dad's shoulder, and my dad put his hand on Ye Ye's and squeezed back. And there was no need for either of them to talk, because just like me and Ye Ye, they understood each other perfectly.

After gifts, there were speeches, toasts, and a cake decorated with white cream and strawberries and kiwis on top. The adults talked and laughed, and I sometimes sat with them, but other times ran around with Gwen and Essie.

I got to sit with Auntie Eva, too, who I haven't seen in so long. She let me feel when the baby kicked, and she told me all about the nursery they're decorating, and how she wants me to be my new cousin's Official Librarian, and she promised that she wouldn't buy any books for the baby's room until I sent her a list of recommendations.

And it was funny, because thinking about a brand-new cousin made me think about how much time had passed, and how I've maybe changed too. I'm not that much taller (sadly). But I'm also different, in other ways. Which I didn't really notice until Ye Ye, from across the table, grabbed the armrests of his chair to pull himself up, and Auntie Eva pushed her chair back, like she was about to jump up.

"Oh, don't," I said. She turned to me, surprised.

"Don't help unless he asks," I explained. "He's still Ye Ye—he can do things for himself."

She looked at me with funny smile.

"How did you get so grown-up?" she asked.

"I don't know," I said with a small smile, feeling my cheeks get a little red, because this was a BIG compliment. "Ms. Clutter, my school librarian, says I'm an Old Soul," I said. "So maybe that's it."

"I think she's right," Auntie Eva said, giving me a kiss on the cheek.

"Well"—I shrugged—"I don't really know what an Old Soul is, so I guess I can't be THAT impressive."

Nai Nai came over to sit with us too. We talked

and laughed and made faces at Essie, who was sitting across from us with my dad next to Ye Ye. So we had a clear view, when Gwen came toddling over to Ye Ye.

She held Batman.

Ye Ye took him, looking very happy, like he thought it was another gift. Then he went "Whooosh!" And Batman flew, up and up, landed on Gwen's ear with full Batman sound effects, booped her nose, and then flew straight onto Ye Ye's head. "Ta-da!!!" Ye Ye said.

The room was busy and loud, but I could still hear, from across the table, as Gwen opened her mouth.

"Silly!" she shrieked, in her loudest, happiest voice. "Why are you Silly?!" She giggled.

And then, a voice spoke. A new, deep, loud voice.

"Becaws he's Ya Ya!" Essie said.

"Hey," my mom said.

"Finally," my dad said.

"Great answer, Essie!" I said. "A-plus."

"Hm." Gwen frowned. Then, "He's *my* Ye Ye."

"No, my Ya Ya!" Essie boomed, trying to scramble onto Ye Ye's lap, as Gwen did the same.

"Uh-oh," my mom said.

Luckily, Grandpa Jenkins came over and let Gwen play with his bow tie, which distracted her from the fight, which I'm guessing is going to be a BIG Theme from now on.

Nai Nai and I smiled at each other and shook our heads like we didn't approve (we did).

"So Silly," I said.

"Ay yah," Nai Nai said. "Some things never change."

"No," I said, leaning into her shoulder with a happy sigh. "I guess they don't, do they?"

She put her arm around me, and I put mine around her, and we watched Gwen and Essie laugh and giggle and say "Play with me, Ye Ye!" and "Again!" and "Bow tie!" and "Silly!" as Ye Ye played peeka-boo and Grandpa Jenkins made funny faces.

"Oh, Cilla," my dad said, coming to sit by me. "Uncle Gerard was just telling me that there's a children's beginner's Cantonese class this summer, if you're interested. The only thing is you'd have to start in a younger class. But he says that you can be the teacher's helper, if you'd like that."

"*What?*" I gasped. My dad put a hand on my shoulder.

"Cilla, sweetie, you don't have to go. Maybe next they'll offer older classes, or—"

I looked at him with big eyes.

"I'm going to be THE BABYSITTER for an ENTIRE CLASS?!" I said. "When does it start? This is going to be the BEST SUMMER EVER!"

"Oh," my dad said. "Right." And then he smiled along with me. "Yes—it will be."

Before we left, we made sure to take photos right in front of the giant gold-and-red dragon on the wall of the restaurant.

"Smile!" Dad said, as the camera clicked, and we all stood there: me, my mom, Gwendolyn, Essie, Nai Nai, Ye Ye, Auntie Eva, Uncle Paul, and Grandma and Grandpa Jenkins.

"Now one with you, Nathan," my mom said.

"Wait, I just want to play with the camera angle," he said.

"Ay yah," Nai Nai said, grinning at me. "Artists are so picky."

"It's true." I nodded. "Also, while you test, can we take a Silly picture, Dad?"

"Yes!" he said. So we did, with tongues sticking out and making faces.

"Another!" Ye Ye said. "A . . ." he looked for the word, and then posed instead, puffing his chest out and putting his arms by his side.

"Batman!" Gwen said, clapping.

"YES, Ye Ye!" I said with a gasp. "A HEROIC one!"

"Wow," Uncle Paul said. "It runs in the family." And then, "Let's do it!"

My dad gave the camera to Auntie Stella and raced to be in the picture too.

So that's how we ended the evening. My whole family, posed in front of the dragon in the Chinese restaurant. My dad standing like Superman, holding Gwen, who waved Batman in the air; my mom and Essie raising their fists; my Nai Nai and Grandma and Grandpa Jenkins pretending they could fly; Auntie Eva and Uncle Paul pretending they were fighting in a superhero battle. And there, at the head of the dragon, were me and my Ye Ye, Ye Ye posed with his cane in front of him, facing off with the dragon like the cane was a sword while he held on to my shoulder with the other hand for balance. And I, Cilla Lee-Jenkins, future author extraordinaire, stood next to him, my hands outstretched, fending off the dragon with him, my best, fiercest, most Epic face on.

We made a great team.

Because my Ye Ye, as it turns out, is a hero, just the way he is.

And so am I.

Which is a stupendous, legendary, supercalifragilisticexpialidocious thing to have in common.

And an Epic end to our story after all.

AFTERWORD

My story is almost over.

But we all know it isn't.

Even if there is only a little more in this particular book.

We drove Ye Ye and Nai Nai home at the end of the night and went upstairs to help unpack their gifts.

And we were all tired.

So when we got there, we marked the occasion the only way we know how.

But don't worry.

There will be more from all of us.

From me, Cilla Lee-Jenkins, future author

extraordinaire; from Gwendolyn Lee-Jenkins, future dance legend; from Essie Lee-Jenkins, future painting prodigy; and from Ye Ye, Nai Nai, Grandma Jenkins, Grandpa Jenkins, Mom, and Dad, and Daisy.

And of course, from Batman.

Who knows how to watch over his family,

And knows how to end a story.

GLOSSARY:
CILLA'S GUIDE TO AN EPIC VOCABULARY

Drama:

When you make something into as big a deal as possible. So, for example, when Gwen jumps on my stomach, I could just say "Oof," which is a normal reaction. But, I could also be Dramatic and yell, "Alas, I am slain!!" And then I pretend to perish, and she giggles, and it's really fun.

Epic:

This is the most exciting kind of story there is. Epics involve Adventures and Quests, and usually you have to go on a long journey on a boat or in a spaceship or on the back of a flying horse. Epics have lots of Struggles and Trials, which can be hard. But they always end in Triumph and Victory (which is a BIG relief!).

Foe:

A bad guy or enemy. Also a Synonym for Villain.

Haiku:

A poem with five
Beats in a line, then seven,
Then five. Just like this!

Nonfiction:

When you're writing about facts, which means the things you're talking about really happened. So for example, when I tell Colleen the story of how Essie chewed on the corner of my notebook and made it all mushy, that's unfortunately nonfiction because how was I to know she'd pull it out of my bag when I left it on the floor?

Metaphor:

When you compare two things that aren't really alike and don't use "like" or "as." So, I could say, "Daisy's bark is music to my ears" (which is true for me, less so for my dad). Or I could say, "Melissa is a star" (which is true for everyone, because she is).

Nai Nai:

The Chinese word for "grandmother." This is pronounced "Nigh Nigh," like if you were saying "sigh sigh" (which my Nai Nai does a lot, especially when I try to help clean up but get distracted and build a teacup tower instead of doing the dishes).

Simile:

When you compare two things using "like" or "as." So "Ms. Clutter is as strong as a mountain" (probably true). Or "Zebulon 5's three suns sparkle like giant glowing disco balls."

Synonym:

A word with the same meaning as another. So I could say that Essie's diaper "smells," or I could use synonyms and say it "reeks," or is "odorous," or "made me run out of the room gasping for fresh air." All of these say the same thing but use different words to do it.

Ye Ye:

The Chinese word for "grandfather." This is pronounced "yeh yeh," like "heh heh" (which is, incidentally, how Villains and Foes sometimes laugh).

AUTHOR'S NOTE

I was much younger than Cilla when my Ye Ye had his stroke—in fact, I was only three and a half years old. But my Ye Ye's stroke forms some of my first vivid memories. I remember the hospital visits, and the worry, and most of all, the differences in my Ye Ye before and after. My Ye Ye always used a cane after his stroke, and he couldn't lift us up and spin us around like he used to, or run with us on the playground. But he found other ways to be there for me and my sisters. From hallway races that he'd referee, to long games of Chinese checkers, to sitting together and reading the English-Chinese newspaper—him reading the Chinese section, me reading the English—we found ways to be together and understand each other, from the silly to the serious.

After his stroke, my Ye Ye continued to serve the community where he'd built his American home and career. Even in his seventies and eighties, he was a frequent figure in Boston's Chinatown, visiting anyone who needed help, counsel, or even just company.

My Ye Ye had another stroke, more than a decade later. I was older then, and these experiences, coupled with my earlier memories, form the basis for many of Cilla's feelings in this story. This second stroke didn't affect his English as much as his mobility. But even then, he was still making jokes, telling stories, and having us sneak him his favorite Chinese dishes.

My Ye Ye passed away many years ago, after living to a very old age. And, as I finished writing this Cilla book, I decided to reread his memoirs (he wrote them in Chinese a few years after his initial stroke, and my cousin, aunt, and mom all banded together to translate them to English).

Imagine my surprise when, as I read his account of his first stroke, I found a whole paragraph about a painting I'd made for him. We lived far away from my Ye Ye and Nai Nai at the time, so during a phone call in his early hospital days, I'd told him I had a "special surprise" for him. My Ye Ye wrote: "Her words made me wonder for days as to what this special gift would be and this thinking helped me to pass the time when I couldn't fall asleep in the quiet room." Later, he devoted a whole paragraph to the painting made by three-and-a-half-year-old me, from the name he gave it: "Autumn Leaves on the River Banks" to the way "the water seemed to be moving and reflected the bright red color of the leaves."

Even now, in my adult life, my Ye Ye is still leaving me gifts: letting me know that just being there for him, in the only way I knew how, was a lasting act of love.

It can be hard to know what to do when the

people we love are affected by something like a stroke. But it's important to know that you're allowed your own feelings, whether they're feelings of worry, sadness, anger, or anything in between. There are people around you who can offer you support, from your family to your friends to your teachers and librarians (who, let's face it, are all probably superheroes in disguise).

And, most of all, know that sometimes, the greatest gift you can give someone else is just being there for them. The simple fact of you—in all your Struggles, Fuhstrations, and Triumphs—is an Epic story, and Epic gift, all on its own.

The Cilla Lee-Jenkins series is semiautobiographical, which means it's based in part on my own life and family. So I thought it would be fun to show you pictures of some of the real, live people who inspired Cilla and her adventures!

Like Cilla, I was bald as a baby, and for quite some time as a kid. This is one of the earliest pictures we have of me—check out the Chinese baby outfit my Nai Nai and Ye Ye got me!

This is a picture of me with my parents when I was about seven months old.

This is a picture of me with my Nai Nai and Ye Ye. In this photo, I'm wearing my first ever cheongsam, which is what the stories in *Future Author Extraordinaire* are based on.

These are my grandparents, who are the inspiration for Grandma and Grandpa Jenkins! In real life, my grandmother also has a PhD and is a professor of art history. My grandfather, like Grandpa Jenkins, wears bowties, is the best lawyer in the business, and LOVES baseball.

This is me as a baby with my E-Pah, which is the Chinese term for great-aunt. E-Pah was my Nai Nai's older sister, and her name was, in fact, Priscilla Lee!

My aunt, uncle, and cousins are the inspirations for Auntie Eva and Uncle Paul, and all the fun and love they show Cilla.

These are two of my best friends growing up—Ben and Courtney. They were the inspiration for Ben and Colleen, and as you can see from this photo, we had A LOT of fun together!

This is me and my friend Annalee. We were the Harry Potter books for Halloween, just like Cilla and Colleen were Selena Moon in *Future Author Extraordinaire*.

When my youngest sister was born—the one who Essie is based on—we spent a lot of time in the hospital. A lot of *The Epic Story* is based on memories of playing in the hospital, and here you can see my other sister (the Blob) and I playing dress up. The nurses were very nice to us (and gave us a lot of costume material, and of course, TONS of popsicles).

This is one of the pictures that the photo described at the end of this book is based on! The one with her hands in the air is The Blob, and the youngest one with the baseball is who Essie is based on.

ACKNOWLEDGMENTS

It's hard to believe that Cilla is drawing to a close and harder still to name all the very many people who have made this series possible. Given the themes of this book, it feels appropriate to begin with a giant thank-you to the librarians in my life. Thank you to the real, live Ms. Clutter who noticed a shy girl in the library every morning and began asking her questions about what she was reading and what she'd recommend. And thank you to all the many librarians, teachers, and educators who have gifted me with their time, care, and superhero powers.

The fact that Cilla exists on the page for everyone to read is thanks to the efforts of the incredible team of people who have accompanied me on this journey. Thank you to Dan Lazar, the most wonderful agent, for your constant faith and advocacy. Thank you, too, Torie Doherty-Monro.

It's hard to find words for my deep gratitude to Connie Hsu, who has brought Cilla so far, taught me so much, and who brings such insight and fun to the writing process. Huge thanks to Megan Abbate, who answers all my questions and cheers me on continuously, and Mekisha Telfer for her work on this book. Thank you, too, to Mary Van Akin, Lucy Del Priore, Melissa Croce, and the fabulous team at Macmillan.

I am indebted to Dana Wulfekotte for bringing Cilla to life. It still feels like she's reached into my head and plucked out exactly what I was seeing. Her insight and compassion shine through in every illustration.

Thank you to my UMass community. Thank you to Jes, Lynn, and Susan, the best dinner crew. And thank you to Louise and Timothy, the most encouraging of office neighbors and friends. Thank you to the Writers Room of Boston, Debka, Alexander, and so many others.

Thank you to my friends, old and new, who have been with me throughout this process. Thank you to Hannah, Yanie, and Ashley. Thank you to Ben, Courtney, Colleen, Laura S., Melissa, Patrick, and Annalee. Thank you to Becky and Kate, who make Boston home, and to Valerie, Erica, Perri, Emily J., and Emily R. A huge thank-you, too, to all my writer friends: to Marika, Debbi, Rob, Katie S., Jarrett, Katie B., Lisa, Sarah, Karen, Elly, and so many more.

To my family: Your love has meant the world and is the substance this book is made of. Thank you to my mom, who is brilliant, beautiful, and fierce in everything she does. Thank you to Grandmom, who sets an example for everything from cooking a great risotto to getting a PhD. Thank you to Catherine and Sarah, the best of sisters. Thank you to Nai Nai, whose warmth I will always carry with me. Thank you to E-Pah, DeDe, Enoch, and the family who watches over me. Thank you to Dr. B., for your gentle wisdom and guidance. Thank you to Auntie Esther, Jenn, Yvonne, Kimmy, Mike, Paul, Jeff, and Ezra, Noah, Rachel, Jeremy, Emmett, and Elly. Thank you to Ethan—hanging out and discovering our shared love of all things *Hamilton*, horror, and Stephen King has been the best—and to Martina.

And finally, thank you to the people this book is dedicated to—Dad, Bobby, Ye Ye, and Uncle Paul. I am so lucky to have you all—you look out for me, teach me, and accept me for all the parts of myself (even the part of me that still has no clue what's happening when a baseball game is on). Uncle Paul, you are such an example and such a model of family and strength. Ye Ye, this book is shaped by the love, kindness, and compassion you modeled every day. You taught me that love, faith, and trust can surmount any difference—be it a difference of religion or, for much of our lives, the different languages we spoke. Bobby, our walks together and the stories you tell are some of my most treasured things. Your warmth, care, and humor set an example for me to follow, and I am in awe of your intelligence, your voice, and the ways in which you embrace change, and change others as a result.

And to Dad, thank you for being the best of dads and teaching me that it's okay to be anything from silly to a rebel and everything in between. Thank you for teaching me to see beauty and craft in every sky, and showing me that I was strong and capable enough to climb the highest ladder safely. Your love for your art and love for your family make me who I am today.